**THEIR LOVE WAS FORBIDDEN,
BUT THEY WERE POWERLESS TO STOP IT**

Lorabeth looked up at Cam's face, illuminated by the newly risen moon, searching hers for an answer. Her resistance melted and she lifted her lips once more for his kiss.

"Don't you know now, Lorabeth?" he whispered softly as he cradled her gently. "Whatever it takes—time, tact, patience—I will practice it, learn it, pray for it. It is worth whatever I have to do. Because it's you I love, and you I must have!"

In his arms she felt cherished, protected. Against her breast she could feel the heavy beat of his heart. She sighed, feeling the strength of his arms enfolding her.

If for this kiss alone, Lorabeth had traveled thousands of miles—if only for this one moment of happiness, she would gladly have traveled ten thousand more.

∽

Also by Jane Peart

Valiant Bride

Look for these other titles
in the *Brides of Montclair* series

Fortune's Bride
Folly's Bride

Published by HarperPaperbacks

Ransomed Bride

BOOK TWO OF
THE BRIDES OF MONTCLAIR SERIES

JANE PEART

Zondervan Books
HarperPaperbacks
Divisions of HarperCollinsPublishers

HarperPaperbacks   *A Division of* HarperCollins*Publishers*
10 East 53rd Street, New York, N.Y. 10022

A trade paperback edition of this book was published in 1989 by Zondervan Books, a Division of HarperCollins*Publishers.*

Cover illustration by Rick Johnson.

First HarperPaperbacks printing: March 1994

Printed in the United States of America

HarperPaperbacks and colophon are trademarks of HarperCollins*Publishers*

❖10 9 8 7 6 5 4 3 2

To all the readers
of Valiant Bride *who asked:*
"And then what happened?"
this book is gratefully dedicated

Chapter 1

"**P**lease, Captain, could you tell me where I might get the next stage to Williamsburg?"

Amos Dagliesh, master of the sailing vessel the *Galatea* turned his sea-weathered face to his questioner, one of the passengers on the ship that he had just brought safely across the Atlantic from England to the Virginia colony.

A frown deepened the line between his bristling, brick-red brows as he reluctantly took his attention from overseeing the unloading of cargo to the slender young woman looking at him with dark, anxious eyes.

He regarded her intently for a moment before answering.

The rose-lined bonnet that she was wearing framed a rounded oval face with a porcelain pink complexion. She had a small arched nose with tiny flared nostrils and her parted mouth, rosy and sweet, revealed pearly teeth.

He had been curious about her the whole trip. She had been a late arrival, boarding the ship with only an hour to spare before they had sailed. During the long journey she had kept to herself, never mingling with the handful of other passengers. Her ticket, identifying her as Miss Dora Carrington, had entitled her to one of the few single cabins and there she had remained, emerging only for meals and a twice-daily walk around the deck.

Their crossing had been fairly smooth, except for a few stormy days mid-ocean. Although several of the passengers had been seasick, the young woman had proved to be a good sailor.

In one rare instance when he had engaged her in conversation, she had told him she was going to relatives in America. Yet there had been no one to meet her when they docked in Yorktown harbor.

Strange! for such an obviously wellborn

young lady to be traveling such a great distance alone. His frown increased almost to a scowl.

"You'll have to ask at the Inn, miss," he replied. "You'll find it easy enough—just up the hill from the dock. There's a sign. I'd have one of my men escort you, but as you can see, I cannot spare one just now."

The girl straightened her shoulders and looked in the direction he pointed.

"Oh, I didn't expect assistance, Captain," she said quickly. "Thank you just the same. I'm sure I'll find it with no trouble."

A practical Scotsman, Captain Dagliesh was not a man much given to idle curiosity, and yet he found himself following the slim figure of his departing passenger with narrowed, speculative eyes. Though simply dressed, he mused, she held herself like a princess, confident, composed for all her youth. This thought quelled the small prick of conscience he felt in not sending one of his officers to accompany her through the crowded seaport town.

Then some clamor below deck caught his straying attention, and he shrugged and resumed his command.

The object of the captain's speculation felt none of the confidence he had attributed to her. As she descended the gangplank, her heart was thudding within her, her pulses racing. Everything around her was new and frightening. She had never seen black people before, and the sight of the dock hands shouting to each other in an unintelligible lingo as they unloaded cargo was terrifying.

The heat of the Virginia sun this spring morning beat down upon her mercilessly as she picked her way carefully through the cluttered dock, holding her wide skirts with one hand while balancing a small wicker reticule with the other.

At the edge of the dock, she paused uncertainly. Accustomed to the cooler English climate, she dabbed daintily at the moisture on her upper lip with a lace-trimmed handkerchief. Then tucking one straying damp curl back under her bonnet, she squinted in the glaring sunlight toward the long hill she must yet climb.

Behind her loomed the tall ship from which she had just disembarked that for the last six weeks had provided her some small measure of familiarity, security. Ahead lay only an unknown future.

Fighting the tears that threatened, a spontaneous prayer welled up fervently: "O Lord, protect me, lead me, guide me in the way I should go." Her own words—but drawn from her well-learned Scripture. The Psalms had been her sustaining comfort and strength all through this perilous journey.

She bit her lip to keep it from trembling, then shifted her reticule to her other hand and started up the cobblestone street. As she neared the top she saw a rambling, slope-roofed building where a wooden sign swung on a post in front. That must be the Inn where she could obtain the information she needed.

Warm and breathless from the climb, she paused at the top and shielded her eyes against the dazzling sunlight. Looking forward she saw the figure of a stocky man, leaning against the doorframe of the entrance. He glanced up, regarding her curiously as she approached. But his countenance was cheerful, she noted with some relief, and his ruddy-complexioned face seemed kind. Sandy-gray hair was queued carelessly, and he was dressed in a homespun shirt, a worn leather vest, and stained breeches.

At her question about the stagecoach, he replied jovially, "You're in luck, miss. The stage for Williamsburg will be leaving within the hour. They're hitchin' up the team in my stables just now."

"Could I send someone to fetch my trunk off the *Galatea* just docked?" she asked, getting out her little drawstring purse and noting with alarm how light the contents were becoming.

"Shure! I'll send my boy fer it." The man extended his hand slyly.

Quickly she handed him a coin, which he took, fingering it and turning it over, squinting his narrowed eyes. "And in what name should the boy be askin' for the trunk, miss?"

Thus preoccupied, the innkeeper failed to notice her moment's hesitation.

"The captain will know. My belongings are in the name of passenger Dora Carrington," she answered quickly. Then to avoid further questions, she asked, "Is there some place I may wait?"

The man nodded toward the door that stood ajar. "Inside, miss. There's the tap room and the keepin' room."

As she ventured a few steps into the Inn, the sounds of voices raised in raucous laughter assailed her ears. Then the smell of pipe smoke mingled with airless heat, and she instinctively recoiled. The innkeeper looked sheepish for a moment; then eyeing her shrewdly he pointed to a rough-hewn table and bench under a shady tree at the side of the building. "You could sit over there out of the sun, miss, if you'd like."

"Oh, yes, thank you," she sighed gratefully.

"And might you be likin' something to drink whilst you wait?"

"Some tea, perhaps, thank you."

He shook his shaggy head. "No tea, miss. Sorry. Just ale."

She looked surprised. *Of course! How stupid of me!* she thought. *This is America, not England!* A new country, new customs, a strangely unfamiliar dialect, a different climate! She was terribly thirsty after the long walk in the searing heat. She must have something to cool her parched throat. *If ale it must be*— she mentally shrugged.

But when the tankard of foamy, dark brew was placed on the rustic table and she raised it to her lips, the warm, malty smell almost turned her stomach. Gamely she took a sip, but the bitter taste revolted her. She wrinkled her nose in protest. Setting down the mug, she reached instead into her skirt pocket for one of the last of her lemon drops and popped it into her mouth.

At least it was more comfortable out of the scorching sun; good to sit in the leafy shade of the huge tree, to set down her wicker basket, which had become heavier with each step she had taken.

She loosened the satin bow under her chin and let her bonnet fall back, then raised her head so that the breeze rustling the leaves overhead could blow on her face. With one hand she lifted blond bunched ringlets from the nape of her neck, feeling a delightful coolness.

Soon the bustling activity and astonishing sights around the Inn claimed her full attention. On the busy thoroughfare in front, wagons trundled by— some filled with hay, others piled high with produce, still others loaded with braying sheep or squawking chickens. Roughly dressed people milled about, greeting each other or calling to their animals in voices accented with a peculiar soft sibilance quite different from the crisp tones of English country folk. And yet, she had to admit, the entire scene was not unlike that of Market Day in any village at home.

She became as interested in all the proceedings as if she were watching a play. It was not until she saw the stagecoach rattling around the corner that she felt the uneasiness that had become her constant companion since she had ventured out upon this journey.

Unconsciously she murmured her sustaining prayer for protection, from the Psalms: "I will trust and not be afraid," and from Isaiah, the comforting reassurance: "I am the Lord thy God, who leadeth thee by the way thou shouldst go."

The coach had now drawn to a stop in front of the Inn, the horses, stamping and snorting and rattling their harnesses while the driver barked orders.

Shortly the innkeeper appeared, followed by a group of prospective passengers. At first glance it seemed that all her fellow-travelers were to be men. But eventually a lone woman, of portly proportions, moving more slowly than the rest, emerged from the Inn, with a younger man in attendance.

From the look of it, most of the male passengers had been refreshing themselves generously while awaiting the arrival of the coach. There was much jovial bantering among them as the baggage was loaded. The driver, his helper, and the innkeeper hefted the pieces onto the top of the coach, where they were strapped in an ill-assorted heap.

Disturbed when she did not see her small

trunk among them, she left the bench and walked over to join the ragged line forming to board the stage. Anxiously she peered down the steep hill toward the harbor. She could see the mast of the *Galatea,* but no sign of the servant the innkeeper had sent to fetch her trunk.

"Ho there, driver!" called a voice from behind her, and momentarily distracted, she turned to see a tall young man elbowing his way through the crowd. "Say, have you room for one more passenger?"

His voice was deep and pleasant, with the same soft slur in his speech that she had already begun to notice in others here.

"If you don't mind riding with me on the box, sir!" the driver shouted back.

"That's the choice seat, I'd say! I'll take it!" came the laughing response. The young fellow looked around, saw that he had an audience, and broke into a grin, showing square, white teeth in a tanned face. As his glance swept the circle, it rested on her for a long moment.

As their eyes met involuntarily she drew in her breath. A rushing warmth tingled through her to the tips of her toes. She hastily lowered her eyes. But not before she saw the frank admiration in his look and observed how extraordinarily handsome he was with the sunlight glinting on his bare head.

In that brief glance not a detail had escaped her eye. She noted russet-brown hair drawn back from a broad forehead and tied in back with a swallow-tailed black ribbon. Obviously feeling the heat, the young man had removed his jacket and slung it over one broad shoulder. The sleeves of a white linen shirt were rolled up from his wrists, exposing bronzed forearms. His legs in buff-colored breeches were long and muscular, and he wore good, if well-worn, black leather boots.

How big and strong and healthy looking he was! He was a man who obviously spent much time in the saddle and out of doors, she speculated. A farmer's son with the manners and dress of a gentleman? An uncommon combination in England, to be sure, where most gentlemen were pale as women and much given to concern for dress and fopperies.

As their eyes met for that single second, unknown to her, he experienced a puzzling sensation. It came and went so rapidly he thought he might have imagined it, for it was indefinable—a certain quickening of his senses, as though something quite wonderful was about to happen.

But there was no time for contemplation, for in the next moment the coachman's helper was bellowing to the driver below, "Is that all the baggage, then?"

"'Pears so!" the driver shouted back. "We'd best be on our way."

"No, not quite," the innkeeper retorted, with a jerk of his thumb in her direction. "This young lady's luggage hasn't got up from the ship yet."

At once she was the target of several pairs of eyes—some impatient, some curious. She twisted her handkerchief in anxiety and stood on tiptoe to peer down the hill. There at last she saw the young boy from the Inn trudging toward them, a small trunk hoisted over his shoulder.

"Miss Carrington's box, sir!" he panted as he heaved it into the innkeeper's arms.

But the handsome latecomer, who was standing nearby, picked it up easily. Turning to her he gave her a rakish smile and arched an eyebrow. "Is this all, *Miss Carrington?*"

Her face flamed. Perhaps he thought himself clever in initiating an introduction, she fumed silently. Yet she was only too aware that his gaze had fallen on the clearly marked brass initials *LEW* atop the hump-backed leather trunk.

She nodded with as much dignity as she could manage, and replied coolly, "Yes, that is all."

Even as she did so, the familiar stirring of panic rose within her. It must indeed seem peculiar for a young woman to have come so far with so few belongings. If he only knew the full truth of the haste with which she had packed, to say nothing of the circumstances under which she had left. . . .

She returned his direct gaze with a tilt of her chin. She had learned in a very short time neither to explain nor to excuse herself. It was by far the safest way. To answer no more than necessary, to give no more information than required, to be reserved without seeming mysterious and thus arousing suspicion. These were the rules of the dangerous game she was playing.

The moment of tension ended abruptly as the driver climbed up on his box. The horses moved restlessly and the coachman's helper opened the carriage doors.

"All right, folks, let's be on our way!"

"May I assist you?" The young man gave her a little bow and extended his hand with a courtly gesture.

Other passengers waiting to board pressed forward impatiently, so there was nothing to do but to place her small, gloved hand in his large one as she lifted her skirt to take the high step into the coach.

The other woman, already seated by a window, had spread her voluminous skirts and was busily arranging them, chattering to her companion.

The window seat on the opposite side was vacant so the girl sat there, gathering her own skirts close as the other passengers pushed in. The interior was unbelievably cramped and stuffy. She put her head out the open window to catch whatever breeze was possible on this early spring, yet summery, afternoon.

From the window she saw the intriguing young man swing himself gracefully up to the seat by the driver.

"Better close that, miss," came the sharp,

querulous voice of the other female passenger. "Once we get started, the dust will be dreadful!"

She saw that the speaker had pulled a heavy veil over her bonnet, thus protecting her face. Probably an experienced traveler. Since her own knowledge was limited, the girl tried to pull the window shut. But it stuck stubbornly.

As she struggled an oily, masculine voice beside her suggested, "Allow me." And a hand reached past her to yank it closed.

She drew away instantly, recoiling from the aroma of cheap cologne combined with strong drink. Allowing herself a sidelong glance at her fellow passenger, she saw that the man was dressed in the flashy, shoddy style of a commercial peddler. His face was barely inches from her own when a sly smile parted his lips, revealing two rows of badly discolored teeth. She prayed the trip to Williamsburg would be a short one!

After accomplishing his task the fellow must have felt he had earned the right to initiate conversation, for he inquired, "Will you be visiting in Williamsburg long?"

In a low tone she answered her well-rehearsed words, "I am recently bereaved, sir. If you will pardon me, I am not inclined to converse." Delivered in a firm voice, this reply usually discouraged further attempts at discourse, she had discovered.

It had this effect now, she noted with relief. In the enforced intimacy of the crowded carriage, all the other passengers could not fail to hear both question and answer, and an immediate silence descended.

Of course, in a way it was true, she rationalized. Even though her father had been dead these three years, she still keenly felt his loss. She felt a twinge of sadness now, remembering how close they had been. Much closer than she had ever felt to her mother, she recalled with a certain wistfulness.

If her father had not died, everything would have been quite different. Certainly she would not be making this terrifying journey, not be alone in this foreign land, thrust among strangers! She closed her eyes momentarily, fortifying herself with the promise of the psalmist: "The Lord watches over strangers; He keeps the fatherless. . . ." *I must believe that,* she reminded herself. *It is all I have.*

Shortly afterward, they heard the shouts of the driver, urging his team forward. There was a sudden lurch, which sent all the passengers lunging against one another. Then, with a few more jolts, the heavily laden coach began moving and pulled away from the curved apron in front of the Inn. Within a few minutes more, they were clopping through the Yorktown streets toward the outskirts of town.

Thus spared any more questions from the curious, she settled back against the ill-padded seat and looked out the window, absorbing the scenery.

Only a few miles out of Yorktown the vista changed abruptly. Every vestige of civilization seemed to have been left behind. The countryside, while spectacularly beautiful, was almost frightening in its wildness. The forest appeared to have swallowed all but the narrow strip of road upon which they were traveling, and there was not a sign of a house anywhere. She felt a momentary shudder ripple down her spine.

Well, at least she was on the last lap of her long journey, she sighed, with an inner release of tension. To this point everything had gone well, with no mishaps. There were still hurdles, of course— perhaps the most important ones lay ahead. But the imminent danger of being apprehended had passed.

The crucial test awaited her in Williamsburg. But she had had time to prepare. On board ship, through the long days and nights at sea, she had done little else but practice. Now her role was letter-perfect, her lines memorized, her performance polished.

Still she knew she must be cautious, take no small detail for granted. It would be so very easy to make the fatal slip that would betray her daring charade. For a moment her pulse pounded erratically. Gradually, however, her weary body, deprived of rest by sleepless nights and hours of anxious anticipation, was lulled by the swaying motion of the coach, and she slept.

Later—how much later she could not be sure—she was awakened by a restless stirring within the coach and a sense of rising excitement on the part of her fellow passengers.

"We're coming into Williamsburg!"

Already the coach had slowed and the horses' hooves beat out a measured cadence as they made their way through the heart of town. She sat up, blinking, a curious mix of emotions churning within. Pressing her face against the window, she looked out.

Williamsburg! What a busy, active place, pulsating with commerce and with its medley of wagons, carriages, and pedestrians. The town appeared to be as thriving as any market town in Britain, with well-kept shops bearing brightly painted signs declaring their owners to be apothecaries, barbers, wigmakers, milliners. There were bakeries, too, and chandleries, liveries, and leather-goods stores.

"Duke of Gloucester Street!" someone called, and she saw they were entering a tree-lined street of fine brick houses surrounded by trimly clipped hedges and flowering gardens.

The coach finally came to a jarring stop in front of a handsome building, The Raleigh Tavern. Some of the carriages were as elegant as any she had seen on the streets of London, and the people as stylishly dressed. She had heard the Colonies spoken of disparagingly by some people she knew, like the Fairchilds, and the headmistress at school, and some of her mother's friends. But, surely, they had never visited this splendid town, or they would have known otherwise.

Suddenly her throat went dry. She was here at last! The end of her long journey, undertaken in reckless haste. The next few hours would decide her fate.

Chapter 2

Her heart hammering wildly within her breast, she alighted from the coach and looked dazedly.

"Will it be possible to obtain lodgings here?" she overheard one of the passengers inquire of a servant who was helping unload luggage.

"Can't be sure, sir. Some of the Burgesses are coming into town early for the opening of the Assembly. You'll have to ask inside."

Indeed, the tavern seemed to be a hub of activity. She watched a constant flow of prosperous-looking gentlemen arrive, descend from fine carriages, then, deep in animated conversations, enter the doorway over which was mounted a lead bust of the illustrious Sir Walter for whom the establishment was named.

Most of her fellow passengers had already joined the throng mounting the steps into the Raleigh and were off in search of refreshment or a night's lodging. Waiting for her trunk to be brought down, she stood uncertainly, wondering what she should do next.

The young man who had assisted her earlier swung down from his place beside the driver and gave her an inquiring glance. He paused for a moment as if debating whether or not to speak. Then, as if thinking better of it, gave her a sweeping bow, put his tricorne on his head, and went whistling down the street. She had heard him tell the coachman he was going to get his own horse, stabled at the livery while he had been in Yorktown.

"This yours, miss?"

She turned to see the driver holding her small trunk.

"Yes."

"Should I carry it in yonder?"

She hesitated, then asked, "Might I leave it with you until I can send someone for it later?"

"Yes, miss," he nodded and thrust forward an outstretched palm. "There's a keepin' fee, o' course."

"Of course," she murmured. There was no way but to give him a coin, further diminishing her meager nest egg. She certainly could not lug the trunk with her on her mission. She opened her purse, hoping the fellow was honest and would not pocket it for himself.

"It will be safe 'til you call for it, miss," he assured her with a beaming smile, and she wondered if she'd overpaid him. Ah, well, it couldn't be helped. In the whole scheme of things, it made little difference. What mattered was what kind of reception would be hers when she made her contact.

The afternoon shadows were lengthening as she started down the shady street toward the neighborhood to which she had been directed. The pleasant, tidy look of it seemed oddly familiar— perhaps because it had been described to her so often. She walked slowly, glancing from one side of the road to the other. The houses were painted white or yellow or blue, with slanting roofs and dormer windows shuttered in contrasting colors. Brightly blooming gardens flourished behind neat picket fences or boxwood hedges.

Then, quite suddenly, she saw it. She would have known it anywhere, she thought with a little catch of breath. Would have recognized it from a hundred dreams. She moved closer, read the little lettered sign on the gate, THE BARNWELLS, and a rush of tears stung her eyes.

With her hand on the gate latch, the panic she had known in small, frantic moments all day clutched her now. This was the time of decision—to turn back or to take her chances.

She took time to still her quavering heart, to breathe a silent prayer, "Be with me now, Lord. I need Thee more than ever!"

Remembering what awaited her in England if she faltered now, she lifted the latch resolutely, pushed open the gate, and walked up the flagstone path to the house. At the fan-lighted front door she paused once again. Then with a trembling hand, she raised the polished brass knocker and let it fall twice.

Behind it she heard the sound of footsteps, the rustle of skirts on a polished floor. Then the door opened and a handsome, rosy-cheeked lady with silver curls escaping a ruffled cap, stood before her. She was plump and dressed in lavender silk with a frothy lace fichu and ruffled sleeves. Snapping blue eyes sharply regarded the pretty young woman on her doorstep, taking in every detail of the stranger's gray, pink-lined bonnet, the plain but stylish merino traveling dress and pelisse. A puzzled frown puckered her smooth forehead, for she knew almost everyone in Williamsburg and she had never seen this girl before.

"Yes?" she asked briskly.

Overcome with nervousness the girl's mouth went dry.

"Yes, my dear?" the woman repeated more gently, seeing the visitor's evident distress. "May I help you in some way?"

With great effort the girl, swallowing hard, cleared her throat, "A—are you the lady of the house?"

"I'm Elizabeth Barnwell," she said, nodding.

"I—I am Lorabeth. Lorabeth Whitaker. Winnie's daughter. *Your* granddaughter."

There was a moment of stunned silence. Then a startled intake of breath, followed by a cry of "Oh, my word! It can't be! And yes! Yes, I do believe—oh, my dear! However did you get here?" Betsy Barnwell took a step backward. "Laura!" she called, "Laura, come here at once!" Then she held out her arms to the girl still standing at the door. "My very dear child! Come in, come in!"

With that she was caught to Betsy's soft bosom, enveloped in the delightfully combined fragrances of rose sachet, starch, and fresh linen. She was hugged hard. Then Betsy gently held her at arm's length and cocked her head.

"Let me look at you! My, how pretty you are! But you don't look a bit like Winnie! Oh, dear me, what a shock—but what a lovely surprise. I must hear everything—how you came, when, and all about it. How is your dear mother? We hardly ever hear from her!" Her arm about Lorabeth's waist, Betsy led her farther into the wide, center hall. As she did, she called, "Laura! Come at once! You'll never guess!" She shook her head, her curls bobbing. "But Winnie was never much for letter writing. Oh, my dear girl, I cannot tell you how I've longed to see my granddaughter all these years. We kept hoping Winnie would come home for a visit and bring you but—Laura! See here! Winnie's own child, all the way from England!"

Lorabeth heard a rustle of taffeta along the hallway, and the slim figure of another woman came hurrying forward toward them.

"It's Lorabeth, Winnie's little daughter!" Betsy exclaimed.

The lovely woman, her blond hair silvered at the temples, held out both hands and smilingly greeted Lorabeth. In the flurry of excitement, of explanations and delighted laughter, the three of them interrupted each other with fragments of sentences and startled gasps.

"We're just about to have tea, my dear. And you must be exhausted after such a journey. Let's go in and you'll tell us all about it," Betsy said, still holding one of Lorabeth's hands as she drew her into the parlor.

The room into which Betsy Barnwell led Lorabeth was bright with late afternoon sunshine. She had the impression of quiet elegance—pale blue walls, masses of fresh flowers, graceful polished furniture. Over the lovely white-panneled fireplace hung a portrait of a bewigged, portly, rosy-cheeked gentleman.

Betsy took a seat on a small, high-backed sofa covered in floral needlepoint and patted the cushion beside her as she beckoned Lorabeth to sit next to her.

"While your Aunt Laura goes to fetch another cup and tell Essie to brew more tea, we'll have a nice catching-up chat. Mercy! I can still scarcely believe you're really here. You don't know how we've conjectured about you, my dear, wondering what you looked like and—Winnie never so much as sent a miniature!" Betsy sighed. She shook her head in exasperation. "But, that's Winnie. . . ." Her voice trailed away significantly. Then she placed her hand over Lorabeth's. "But enough of that. Let's talk about *you*, my dear!"

Betsy paused to take a breath while regarding Lorabeth with rather puzzled scrutiny.

"There's not a bit of family resemblance that I can see! Winnie was fair, of course, but the features—take off your bonnet, dear," Betsy directed.

Obediently Lorabeth untied the ribbons under her chin, let her shovel bonnet fall back, and put up one fragile hand to smooth her pale blond hair.

"Now, I want to know how it is you came to travel all this way alone? The last we heard from your mother, you were off at boarding school and she had taken a position as housekeeper to some fine family in the country after your father died— the Fairchilds of Kent, wasn't it?"

Just then Aunt Laura came back into the room, followed by a black woman wearing a blue, stiffly starched apron, bright calico dress, and white turban. The woman was carrying a tray, which she set on the round table behind which Laura had seated herself. Then she turned a frankly curious gaze on Lorabeth.

"Essie," Betsy addressed her, "can you believe this pretty child is Miss Winnie's daughter, all the way from England?"

Essie grinned at Lorabeth and bobbed a curtsy. "Pleased to meet ya, Missy. No'm," she shook her head. "She sure doan 'semble her mama, do she? But she mahty pretty jes' de same."

Lorabeth smiled and murmured a polite "thank you." But she was greatly surprised by the familiarity between mistress and servant. Certainly this friendly exchange would not have been countenanced in the Fairchild household, where even the housekeeper was treated with haughty condescension. Even in their own small cottage, Mama ordered their little maid of all work, Lilly, about without a thought for her opinions. How different it was here in the Colonies, Lorabeth mused.

"Here, dear." Aunt Laura handed Lorabeth one of the eggshell thin cups into which she had poured the fragrant, steaming tea, then said to her mother, "Now, Mama, let us allow Lorabeth to have her tea in peace, not ply her with questions. She must be tired from her trip—and hungry, too."

"Quite right, my dear," Betsy agreed, and after urging Lorabeth to help herself to the plentiful delicacies, she turned her attention to her own tea and well-filled plate.

Lorabeth sipped the deliciously hot, aromatic tea, feeling its gentle stimulation gradually penetrate her lightheadedness. The feeling of dread that had oppressed her since entering the Barnwell house, the fear of being rejected had been quickly dispelled by the warmth of her welcome within this cordial atmosphere.

When she tasted the spicy nutbread and freshly churned sweet butter, Lorabeth realized how hungry she was. She had eaten nothing since the ship's breakfast of hardtack and watery tea. During the last two weeks aboard the *Galatea,* the meals had become monotonous repetitions. Slowly Lorabeth's healthy appetite and good spirits revived.

Soon Betsy's irrepressible curiosity reasserted itself and she resumed her questioning.

"It is still hard for me to believe you are really here, dear child. It has long been my desire to have you for an extended visit. In fact, I wrote your mother several times to allow you to come to us— after your father's death, for instance." She paused for a moment to replenish Lorabeth's plate with strawberries the size of small plums, then hurried on. "I'm sure things weren't easy for Winnie or for you, either, after your father's untimely death. The house the school provided for the headmaster had to be given up for his replacement, your mother said in one of her infrequent letters. So, at that time, I strongly urged her to come back to Virginia—make her home here with us! But . . ." Again Betsy shook her head sorrowfully.

"Mother!" Aunt Laura admonished gently, as if to warn her to abandon this line of conversation.

But Betsy ignored her. "Why didn't your mother come with you?" she persisted.

"She has a very responsible position with the Fairchilds, Grandmother. They depend on her. Especially since old Mr. Fairchild's stroke—"

"But why ever did she allow you to come so far alone?"

This was the moment, above all others, that Lorabeth had most dreaded—to be confronted with the reason she had undertaken this journey alone. In the class of society to which the Barnwells belonged, such a thing was rarely done and then only under the most extreme circumstances.

Even though Lorabeth had rehearsed her reply dozens of times, as she looked into those blue eyes gazing at her with such affectionate concern, her throat constricted painfully. Her face felt hot, her hands grew clammy, and she was suddenly tongue-tied.

It was Aunt Laura who rescued her—at least temporarily—for she rose and chided her mother laughingly. "Mother, dear, isn't it enough that Lorabeth is here! No matter how or why! Let us give her a reprieve from all these questions.

"I'm sure Lorabeth would like to go up to her room, Mama, and freshen up, perhaps even lie down for a rest before dinner." Turning to Lorabeth, she said, "We'll send our boy, Thaddeus, to the Raleigh for your trunk right away."

"That's very kind. If you're certain I'll be no trouble—"

"Trouble!" exclaimed Betsy, thoroughly shocked. "*Trouble? my own granddaughter,* my own flesh and blood, under my roof for the first time, *trouble!* I should say not! A *pleasure,* my dear child! An undreamed of pleasure! Now you go along. Laura will take you upstairs to the room your own dear mama had when she was a girl. We'll have plenty of opportunity to visit, for I intend to keep you for a long time!"

Lorabeth followed Aunt Laura out to the hallway and up the curved stairs to the second floor. At the end of the upstairs hall Laura opened the door to an airy, spacious room.

"Here you are, dear. Essie will bring up hot water and clean towels later. Why don't you lie down and try to get a little nap. We don't dine until eight. And I'm afraid Mama has quite worn you out with all her questions. Don't let it bother you. She is so delighted you're here, as am I. We'll probably both spoil you!" she said with a light laugh. Then kissing Lorabeth on both cheeks she went out, closing the door quietly behind her.

Lorabeth let out the breath she had been holding, in a long sigh of relief. Although managing to evade her grandmother's direct question for now, she knew there would come a time when she could no longer avoid giving the answer she had prepared so carefully.

Her reprieve was only temporary. Inevitably would come the day of reckoning.

Like one in a trance, Lorabeth moved to the middle of the room and looked around. Everything was so bright, so fresh and delightful. Crisp, flowered chintz flounces on the tester of the four-poster bed matched the deep dust-ruffle along the bottom; a white crocheted coverlet and white muslin curtains at the windows accentuated the airiness. A high armoire and kidney-shaped dressing table were of mellow golden maple. There was a wing-chair and stool opposite a little writing desk on either side of the fireplace; on the washstand, a bowl and pitcher of rose-painted china.

It was all very different from the surroundings in which she usually found herself. She had grown up in an underpaid headmaster's house, furnished with cast-offs, without color or taste. At boarding school the rooms for "scholarship girls" were as bare as monk's cells, with a narrow single bed, washstand, study desk, and chair.

Suddenly Lorabeth began to tremble. Her knees felt wobbly and she sat down shakily on the small fiddle-back chair next to the door. She clasped her arms around her slight frame, shivering as if from cold. She had not realized how tightly wound every nerve had been until now. She could not seem to stop their quivering.

Almost warily, she glanced around her. It *was* true. She was here. She had gotten this far without a slip. No one had seemed suspicious, manifesting only a natural curiosity occasioned by the strange circumstances of her unexpected arrival. These lovely people—her very own kin—had accepted her easily and simply, with a warmth she had never before experienced.

Wearily Lorabeth closed her eyes.

In spite of all she had endured, she told herself, the long journey to Virginia had been worth the risk. And, whatever the cost, she meant to stay.

Chapter 3

Upon coming down to dinner that evening, Lorabeth was surprised to see that both Betsy and Aunt Laura were elegantly gowned. Virginians, it appeared, enjoyed a more gracious way of life than did the same social class in England, for both ladies had changed from their daytime frocks into more formal attire.

In comparison to Betsy's mauve taffeta and Aunt Laura's lilac silk, her own simple blue merino, though trimmed with fluted linen and edged with cotton lace, seemed almost Quaker-plain.

However, soon caught up in the charming customs of her relatives and her surroundings, Lorabeth did not fret long.

At first she thought the ladies might be expecting company, but when they entered the dining room, softly aglow with candlelight, she saw that the table was set for only three. Lorabeth glanced around with pleasure. The sheen of silver, the gleaming china, the centerpiece of fresh yellow daffodils, all satisfied her inner yearning and appreciation of beauty.

Everything was new and interesting; even the dishes served—especially the assortment of vegetables that Betsy told her were grown in their own garden, and the fluffy mounds of rice she had never tasted before. The succulent chicken and hot breads, too, were delicious and Lorabeth ate heartily.

Thankfully she was not plied with too many questions during dinner; certainly, none requiring careful answers. There seemed to be an unspoken agreement that she should not be pressured on her first night in Williamsburg.

In the gentle atmosphere, Lorabeth began to relax. This house, like all houses, reflected the people who lived in it. She had felt the coldness in the Fairchilds' huge mansion, and the bitter melancholy that haunted the little house she shared with her mother after her father's death. Even when they had lived at the headmaster's house while he was still alive, there had been an indefinable air of tension. Perhaps her mother's constant complaining and dissatisfaction had been the cause or, to be charitable, the reverse.

But here the environment was one of serenity and cheerful order. Undoubtedly Betsy's benevolent personality and Aunt Laura's sweet spirit were responsible for the aura.

Studying Aunt Laura with her lovely cameo-like features, the masses of silvery blond hair, Lorabeth wondered why she still lived at home, why she had never married. Was there some secret sorrow in her past?

As she listened to the two older women softly conversing about friends and local happenings, Lorabeth recalled once again that, back home in England, she had often heard Virginia referred to as an "untamed wilderness of rogues and ruffians." Certainly this description did not take into account the culture and refinement she had found. Strangely even her mother, although born and reared here, never spoke in defense of her homeland.

Just as dessert, a cool lemon sorbet, was being served, there was a loud rap at the front door. Before anyone could answer its summons, the door swung open, admitting someone with a brisk stride and a hearty greeting.

"Hello! Anyone home?"

At the sound of that resonant male voice, Betsy and Aunt Laura exchanged a smile and a knowing look.

"Cameron!" exclaimed Betsy. Winking at Lorabeth, she put a finger to her lips, then called to the unseen arrival, "Come in, dear. We're just finishing dinner."

Lorabeth's back was to the door, so she could not see who now stood there. But for some reason she felt a pang of alarm.

"Sorry if I startled you, Auntie B. And my apologies for barging in like this without an invitation—especially now I see you have company. But I've come to beg pity! I find myself stranded in Williamsburg too late to start back for Montclair. May I stay the night?"

"Too long lingering at Raleigh Tavern, I've no doubt!" Betsy retorted with mock severity. "And of course you never need an invitation here, dear boy. Come—do sit down. I'll have Essie bring another plate. And I want you to see *our* surprise!"

To Lorabeth she said, "My dear, this young rascal is Cameron Montrose." Lorabeth inclined her head slightly as a tall figure strode to the opposite side of the table and made a gallant bow.

When she saw him, she very nearly fainted! It was the same young man who had made the trip on the coach from Yorktown that morning— the one who had boarded late and had ridden beside the driver all the way to Williamsburg.

Her heart leapt into her throat and remained there, pounding violently, preventing her from swallowing or speaking. Her fingertips gripped the edge of the table.

"Cameron, meet your cousin, Lorabeth Whitaker," Betsy said triumphantly.

The young man's eyes widened, one eyebrow lifted.

With a sinking heart, Lorabeth's stomach knotted tightly, remembering he had heard her addressed as "Miss Carrington" when her trunk was brought up from the ship. Would he expose her? Demand to know why she had traveled under an assumed name? What she was doing here under his relatives' roof?

"This is your Aunt Winnifred's daughter," Betsy continued.

Cameron bowed, a smile tugging at the corners of his mouth.

"My pleasure, *Cousin* Lorabeth," he said. Then, turning to Betsy, he remarked archly, "This must have come as a great surprise, Auntie B."

"Indeed it did!" Betsy chuckled. "A *far* pleasanter surprise than the one her mother gave us twenty years ago!"

Cameron pulled out a chair and sat down, not taking his eyes from Lorabeth's pale face.

"Ah, yes! Runaway Winnie!" He looked directly across at Lorabeth. "Of course, you probably know that if things had been different, she might have been my mother. Or at least my father's bride. What strange turns life takes, wouldn't you agree—*cousin?*"

Were his eyes twinkling mischievously or was there a hidden threat in their depths? Lorabeth wondered frantically.

"Ring for Essie, Laura, dear. Cameron needs to be fed," Betsy declared.

Laura lifted the silver bell by her glass and gave it a jangle. Essie appeared as if by magic, bearing a plate heaped with chicken, rice, and vegetables, and placed it with a smile before Cameron.

It was clear he was a favorite with both servants and mistresses of the house.

"So, now, Cameron," Betsy beamed at him fondly, "tell us what brings you to Williamsburg and all the events of your day. Knowing *you*, I've no doubt it has been filled with adventure and interesting encounters."

"*Intriguing* adventure, *unexpected* encounters! Ah, yes, Auntie B., my day was certainly filled with *those*," Cam chuckled. "And surprises as well. None nicer, I might add, than finding I've a cousin I've never met!"

He gave Lorabeth a knowing glance that sent a stiletto of fear into her heart. She twisted her napkin nervously. What if he should recount having seen her in Yorktown, the initials on her trunk conflicting with the name to which she had replied?

But her worst fears were not realized. Cameron led the conversation into other subjects, of people she did not know and of a place called "Montclair." It soon became clear he had no intention of bringing up the fact of their earlier meeting or its puzzling circumstances.

She was aware, however, that his eyes rested often upon her, although with a studied casualness. Whenever his gaze met her own, her breathing became shallow and her pulse raced. How disastrous if she should be found out now—after all she had been through!

In spite of her tension and the long day, Lorabeth felt herself growing drowsy, and her eyelids began to droop. It was Aunt Laura who noticed her weariness and immediately suggested she be excused.

"It's been an exhausting day for Lorabeth," she said in explanation to Cameron as she rose and went to Lorabeth's side, placing her hand gently on her shoulder.

Cameron also got to his feet. Bowing slightly from the waist, he said, "Welcome to Williamsburg and to Virginia, cousin. I hope soon we can also welcome you at Montclair. I'm sure my mother will send an invitation to that effect as soon as she knows of your presence here."

"Yes, indeed. We must have a real reunion!" declared Betsy, bobbing her head in agreement. "Now, run along with Laura, child, and get a good night's sleep. There will be plenty of time later for visiting and getting to know one another."

Aunt Laura lighted her candle and accompanied her to the foot of the stairway. Then, leaning her soft cheek against Lorabeth's, bid her "sweet dreams."

Lorabeth accepted the candle in its brass holder and slowly mounted the steps. At the bend of the staircase, she looked back. Through the dining room door, she could see the three still seated at the table. The low murmur of their voices and the muted sound of laughter floated up to her. A feeling of melancholy longing touched her. To belong to such a family would be a very special thing.

Once in her room she took the candle to the bedside table and began to undress. Her movements were slow and stiff; her limbs weighted by fatigue. She was much too tired to think through the events of the day. For now they remained a muddle, fraught with anxiety and excitement and, yes, with fear.

She could still scarcely believe she was actually in Virginia, in the Barnwell house—welcome, accepted, safe! She looked now at the bed, draped with mosquito netting. Someone had turned down the coverlet, and it beckoned invitingly.

Lorabeth had never been pampered in her life, and now the tenderness with which she was being received brought tears to her eyes. Suddenly she was overwhelmed at the thought of providential protection through all the events of her life that had brought her to this moment, and she sank to her knees beside the high tester bed.

She had already taken her worn little Bible from her trunk. Now she opened it to the Psalms, and by the light of the flickering candle, she read from the 138th: "In the day when I cried thou answeredst me, and strengthenedst me with strength in my soul. . . .Though I walk in the midst of trouble, thou wilt protect me. . . .The Lord will perfect that which concerneth me."

Yes, in the time of her need, He had cared for her, had made the rough way smooth, had opened doors, and had lighted her path. Surely His goodness and mercy had followed her here to Virginia.

"And the Lord shall fulfill his purpose for thee."

Lorabeth believed that with all her heart, and clung to that truth. He would not have let her come so far only to have to return to the horror she had left behind.

It would be all right. Things had a way of working out. In a few days she would talk to Betsy, tell her the whole story, seek her advice, her help. . . .

Lorabeth lay long awake that night in the room that had belonged to her mother. The worst was over, she told herself. The panicky trip from school, boarding the big ship, the long and frightening ocean voyage, the journey from Yorktown to Williamsburg, her meeting with Betsy and Laura—all had gone remarkably well. All except the unexpected appearance of Cameron Montrose and the information that the handsome stranger was her *cousin!*

Ever since she had first set eyes upon him, everything about him had fascinated her—his long-legged height; his Virginia drawl; his slow, enigmatic smile; his easy-going manner; his laugh, so spontaneous, so joyful. There was a reckless vigor about him. She had never known anyone who radiated such a love of life, such energy and enthusiasm.

But she was afraid. What was Cameron really thinking? What did he intend to do?

Perhaps he had already told Betsy and Aunt Laura about their meeting earlier in Yorktown when she had been called "*Miss Carrington!*" No, somehow Lorabeth did not think he had. He could easily have betrayed her when Betsy had introduced her as "Lorabeth Whitaker." There was no reason for him to keep silent. Yet he had. Maybe for reasons of his *own,* he had remained silent.

Whatever those reasons Lorabeth recalled with a sudden breathlessness that, in that very first glance that had passed between them in Yorktown that morning, there had been an instant of something akin to *recognition!* A shock had passed like lightning through her very being when those deep-set blue eyes caught and held hers. She had seen a glimmer of that same look again this evening as those eyes had sought hers again and again during dinner.

Was she mistaken? Could it be only her imagination? Or was there something real, if inscrutable, in those glances? More than curiosity? More than a natural interest of a young man for a pretty girl? It seemed to her, even in that first moment, there had been either a challenge—or a promise.

Had he felt it, too? Was Cameron Montrose as inexplicably drawn to her as she was to him?

Chapter 4

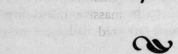

On her first morning in Williamsburg Lorabeth was awakened by Essie, bringing her a tray of tea and biscuits and reminding her that it was Sunday and that her grandmother expected her to accompany them to church.

It was tempting to linger a little longer in the lavender-scented sheets among the soft, smooth linen pillows, but Lorabeth did not give in to the inclination. She washed and dressed quickly, and hurried downstairs.

Her grandmother and Aunt Laura were having second cups of tea when Lorabeth made her entrance into the sunny dining room. Cameron was just helping himself to a generous portion of ham slices and eggs at the massive mahogany buffet, where there were covered dishes of hot breads as well as a crystal bowl of fresh fruit.

They all turned smiling faces in her direction, asked her how she had slept, and urged her to eat a hearty breakfast.

"Church services are at eleven, Lorabeth, so there's no need to rush." Then, indicating feigned disapproval, Betsy said, "Cameron, naughty boy, is not attending with us. Says he has to get started back to Montclair right away."

"It's true, Aunt B!" Cam protested. "You know it's a hard day's ride to Montclair, and if I don't leave soon, it will be nightfall before I reach home. And what news I have to tell once I get there! Lorabeth, have you any idea what an object of curiosity and speculation you have been all these years?" He threw her a teasing glance. As she blushed, he laughed and asked in mock astonishment, "Or didn't you know your mother's running off with her French tutor was the 'scandal of the century'?"

"Now, that's quite enough, Cameron!" reprimanded Betsy. "You're embarrassing Lorabeth. Don't pay him any attention, my dear. He's a frightful tease."

With that remark of dismissal, she turned her attention to Lorabeth's blue woolen gown. "Didn't you bring anything lighter to wear, child? It's almost summerlike today—and I fear you'll be much too warm in that frock."

"I'm sorry, no, Grandmother. England is so much cooler this time of year. . . .I never thought . . ." Her voice trailed off anxiously. "Won't this do?" She was only too aware of her meager wardrobe, but there was little choice.

"Oh, it's charming, my dear. I'm just thinking of later on as the weather gets even warmer."

"Well, if you ladies are going to start talking clothes and fashion, that is my cue," said Cameron, getting to his feet. "I really must be off now, Aunt Betsy. Thank you for your wonderful hospitality, as usual. Goodbye, Aunt Laura. And, Lorabeth, I know my mother will want to have you out to Montclair for a good, long visit very soon."

Cameron kissed his two aunts, made a little bow to Lorabeth, and strode from the room. Aunt Laura went to the window and stood watching his tall figure swing into the saddle of the horse the stable boy had just brought round.

"What a dear boy Cameron is," she said, sighing. "A real charmer, so gentle and yet so strong and manly. A pity, though, about Malinda.

She certainly doesn't deserve such a prize!"

"Who is Malinda?" Lorabeth asked innocently.

"The little minx he's engaged to!" Betsy snapped.

"Malinda Draper. I still don't know quite how it came about. I doubt if Noramary and Duncan do either," Aunt Laura said, shaking her head.

"Her mama, of course!" supplied Betsy. "Felicia Draper knows a good catch when she sees one. She had Malinda paired with Cameron while they were still in their cradles. Remember last year at the Christmas Ball? Malinda had just returned from England with all her airs and the newest fashions. Cameron was quite dazzled and from then on, she held all the cards. But Mama is the one who played them so cleverly."

Lorabeth felt a strange, sinking sensation at these comments from her grandmother and aunt—a feeling of dismay that was totally irrational given her short acquaintance with Cameron. So what if this utterly charming young man was engaged, spoken for, all but married? Why should she suddenly feel so devastated? After all, wasn't he her first cousin? They could never have been anything more than friends, at best.

Lorabeth rode with her grandmother and Aunt Laura to church in an open carriage. Surprised by the warmth of the early morning, she gazed with delight at the beauty of Williamsburg in April. Flowering trees and bushes gave the aura of a pastel painting. The air was perfumed with the scent of many flowers; the day, tinted with pale yellow from row upon row of primroses bordering gardens and hundreds of daffodils peeking from behind the picket fences of houses that lined the road to church. Even the salmon-colored brick of the steepled church itself seemed to glow with mellow light in the glorious sunshine.

As they pulled into the churchyard, the bell was tolling. Grandmother's coachman sprang down lightly and assisted the three ladies from the carriage. Other churchgoers on their way into the service greeted them, including Lorabeth in their friendly smiles and nods, although there was no time for introductions.

Lorabeth settled herself between her grandmother and aunt in the Barnwell family pew just as the rector emerged from the vestry to begin the service.

Lorabeth noted with some surprise and not a little delight the cheerful atmosphere in the church. There were smiles and nods among members of the congregation as they got out their hymnals. The first hymn was joyful in melody and lyric and was sung loudly and enthusiastically—a far cry from the solemn Sundays at Briarwood School chapel, where the hymns were funereal dirges and the sermons long and full of admonitions on wickedness and repentance.

With a great rustling of skirts and adjusting of plumed bonnets, the congregation settled down for the sermon. Lorabeth was curious to hear what kind of message would be given to this pleasant and apparently godly group. To her astonished heart, it spoke directly to her! Or at least that was the way she felt when she heard the cherubic-faced minister's words.

"We are taking our text from Matthew 25 this morning," he said, and proceeded to read from the Gospel of St. Matthew. When he came to the part— "Come, ye blessed of my Father, inherit the Kingdom . . . for I was hungry and ye gave me to eat, I was thirsty and ye gave me drink, I was a stranger and ye took me in"—Lorabeth sent a grateful glance in Betsy's direction and felt unexpected tears.

The service over, Lorabeth followed her grandmother and aunt into the churchyard and was amazed by the holiday air of the after-church crowd. Why, it was like Fair Day in an English village, she thought in surprise, with a great deal of laughter, warm greetings, kisses among the ladies, and hand-pumping among the gentlemen. The whole congregation seemed to linger, unmindful of time, mingling, visiting, gossiping, exchanging news, extending and accepting invitations.

While her grandmother and aunt were busily chatting, Lorabeth noticed the approach of a tall, elegantly dressed lady accompanied by two strikingly handsome young men. The trio was headed right in their direction.

Instinctively Lorabeth stepped back, shielded by her grandmother's bulk, as she heard Betsy exclaim, "Why, it's Jacqueline Cameron and her son, Bracken, but who is the other young man?"

"I believe it's their houseguest, a fellow student of Bracken's," whispered Aunt Laura.

"Good day, Mistress Cameron," Betsy greeted the dark-eyed beauty.

Jacqueline Cameron was one of those fortunate women whose age would forever remain a mystery, mused Lorabeth. Although she was the mother of a grown son, the lady's face was remarkably smooth, her brown eyes sparkled with youthful gaiety, and her smile was as animated as her conversation. Her slender figure and graceful movements were those of a young girl.

"Ah, Mistress Barnwell and Miss Laura! How good to see you." Mrs. Cameron spoke with a slight accent that Lorabeth recognized as French. She embraced the two Barnwell ladies, then turned her lovely smile on Lorabeth.

"My granddaughter has just arrived from England," Betsy proudly made the introduction. "Winnie's daughter, Lorabeth Whitaker."

Mrs. Cameron's eyes widened but she politely suppressed her surprised gasp. "Ah, yes—Winnie! And this is her child! But she doesn't resemble the Barnwell family at all, does she?" Then she smiled reassuringly at Lorabeth, who was beginning to feel uncomfortable under the scrutiny of both Jacqueline and the two young men at her side. "But it is better to be oneself, *n'est ce pas?* To be one of a kind. Not to be compared to anyone else. *Voilà!*"

Jacqueline then lowered one eyelid in a sly wink. With one graceful hand she made a sweeping gesture. "And now may I present these two rascals, who were so restless all during the service, craning their necks, peering over their hymnals, paying no attention at all to the oh-so-profound sermon—for a glimpse of the *très jolie jeune mademoiselle* in the Barnwell pew this morning."

Lorabeth felt her cheeks grow warm at the obvious eagerness of the young men waiting to be introduced.

"My son Bracken and his friend, Blakely Ashford." Bracken had inherited his mother's brunette good looks and was no doubt the handsomer of the two. But to Lorabeth, Blakely had an endearing, boyish charm that was most appealing.

He was tall, almost awkward as he bowed over her hand, holding it longer than etiquette required. His clear blue eyes were as guileless as a child's, and in them Lorabeth saw an immediate worshipful gaze that startled her.

She felt herself flushing under it and turned away to hear Mrs. Cameron ask Betsy, "Does

Noramary know of the little English cousin's arrival? If not, since we are returning to the plantation tomorrow, perhaps I can carry the happy news?"

"She knows by now. Cameron was here only yesterday and left this morning. I'm sure he has lost no time in telling her," Betsy said.

"I hope you will allow me the pleasure of entertaining for this enchanting child at Cameron Hall. I would so much love to give her a party—a ball perhaps? And a midnight supper on the night of the first full moon—*trés romantique, n'est ce pas?*" Jacqueline shrugged her elegant shoulders.

"I am sure we shall see a great deal of each other while Lorabeth is with us," Betsy replied, smiling complacently and noticing the effect Lorabeth had had on the two young gentlemen. That rogue, Bracken, about whom there had been many romantic rumors, was not suitable for Lorabeth, she decided. But young Blakely—now there was a real possibility. The Ashfords were a prominent family, with fine heritage and great wealth on both sides. Neither had Betsy missed the flush that had colored Blakely's face as he bent over Lorabeth's hand. The girl's unique beauty had struck a ready target, if she were not mistaken.

And, of course, in matters of the heart Betsy Barnwell was rarely mistaken.

*   *   *

The next day there could be no doubt of it. A bouquet of lovely spring flowers in a starched lace ruffle was delivered to Lorabeth with a note from Blakely asking for permission to call.

The promised invitation from Montclair was prompt in arriving, also. And as soon as the acceptance was written and dispatched to Montclair, by way of the Montrose servant, Lorabeth witnessed with amazement the unexpected flurry that followed.

Immediately she was summoned to Aunt Laura's sitting room, where her grandmother and aunt began to discuss plans for the visit to Aunt Noramary's plantation home—Montclair.

"Lorabeth, my dear, we must see to replenishing your wardrobe at once! Noramary has many plans. She is giving a gala party to introduce you to society, and of course you will be needing a lovely gown. But that will be just a prelude to a round of parties and other invitations you will receive. The summer season will be starting soon, and you will be attending ever so many festivities for young people. So, come along, we'll take a look through what you have and then decide"—Betsy got up, motioning Lorabeth to follow—"what we must do."

In Lorabeth's bedroom, Betsy marched straight over to the armoire and began taking out Lorabeth's dresses one at a time with a great deal of clucking of her tongue and shaking of her head.

"Oh, this will never do," she declared. "All your things are much too heavy for Virginia summers, my dear. We must do something about it at once. Light muslins, dimities, and voile are all one can be expected to endure in this weather . . . and only two petticoats . . . cotton stockings. . . .We'll pick out some materials this very afternoon and have Madame Luisa make you some dresses right away."

To herself Betsy wondered, *What was Winnie thinking of, to send her daughter off with such a meager supply of suitable clothes? How did she expect her to put her best foot forward in Virginia society without a proper wardrobe?* She had not wanted to hurt the precious child by displaying her indignation and shock. That's why tactfully she used the excuse of the climate.

Meanwhile Betsy's matchmaking mind was spinning with plans. Had she not arranged prestigious marriages for two of her daughters, to say nothing of Noramary? With the exception, of course, of Laura and Winnie—but no matter. Lorabeth had all the necessary qualities of beauty, grace, and charm to launch her into society and Betsy was determined this time not to fail.

Lorabeth was speechless. She had never owned more than three dresses at one time (except for the drab gray school uniform), usually ones cut down from her mother's old ones. She listened in silent wonder as her grandmother and aunt made lists, alternately adding other necessities. Never in her short life had Lorabeth been the subject of so much attention.

From that day until their departure two weeks later for Montclair, her days were crowded with dressmaker appointments, fittings, and shopping tours, shepherded by Aunt Laura. Grandmother engaged the services of Madame Luisa, a fine seamstress in town, to make Lorabeth's new wardrobe. To the impoverished girl, it was a dizzying whirl of activity.

But if her days were filled, her evenings were less so.

Because Blakely Ashford, who had been so flatteringly attentive after meeting her, had left with the Camerons for their plantation home, Cameron Hall, his frequent calls were temporarily suspended. Her grandmother always retired early and Aunt Laura kept busy with the management of the household, often into the evenings. Left to her own devices in the long twilight of the Virginia spring, Lorabeth spent time in the lovely garden, and she found her thoughts often dwelling on Cameron Montrose.

For the time being, she pushed aside the necessity of telling her grandmother and Aunt Laura the real reason she had come to Virginia.

She allowed herself the luxury of living in the present. It would take several weeks yet for any word from England to spoil this idyllic interlude. After all she had been through, Lorabeth justified the postponement, determined to enjoy this most pleasant phase of her life.

She was looking forward to the visit to Montclair, the Montroses' plantation mansion on the James River. She was curious to meet Noramary, who had taken her own mother's place as the bride of Duncan Montrose.

But in her secret heart it was her charming cousin Cameron that, most of all, she wanted to see again.

Chapter 5

Lorabeth's first view of Montclair was through a veil of white dogwood blossoms as the Barnwell carriage made its way up the winding road leading to the Montrose estate. Just as they rounded the bend and entered the gates, the rays of the late afternoon sun touched the treetops surrounding the house, enveloping it in a shining radiance.

The large U-shaped, mellowed brick structure was of simple, even austere architecture. But it evoked a serenity, a dignity, a tranquility that touched the young girl deeply.

Nearing the house Lorabeth's heartbeat quickened. She leaned forward eagerly, aware of a peculiar sensation, a definite feeling of "homecoming."

Lorabeth's first impressions of the Montrose household were both pleasant and puzzling. There was little formality although there were many servants, no ostentatiousness although the surroundings were luxurious. Both Cameron's parents were without pretension. Uncle Duncan, tall, handsome, looking very much the way Cameron might look in thirty years, was quiet, dignified, while Aunty Noramary was warm and vivacious. In spite of what Lorabeth had learned about their arranged marriage, there seemed a deep bond between them. Duncan followed his petite wife's every move with affectionate eyes.

Obviously, in their case, the Scripture verse "All things work together for good to them that love God" had proved true. What had begun as duty had become love.

Guests had been invited from neighboring plantations to meet "the little English cousin," and Lorabeth was almost overwhelmed by this display of "Virginia hospitality." As Grandmother Barnwell had predicted, Lorabeth received many invitations, with promises of follow-up reminders as to date and time and type of event.

Dinner was a sumptuous affair. The long table,

set with gleaming gold-rimmed china and shining silver, seated more than twenty, and the conversation was as sparkling as the crystal.

Cameron arrived only a few minutes before dinner was announced, making the excuse to his mildly disapproving mother that he had ridden to the far end of the plantation that afternoon and had only now returned.

"I abused my horse, I'm afraid, racing to get back by sundown. I wouldn't have missed Lorabeth's first evening at Montclair on any account," he declared with a mischievous grin. "Welcome to Montclair, cousin!"

He bowed gallantly to Lorabeth and raised her fingertips to his lips.

She was struck again with his splendid looks. This, combined with an easy charm, must have a devastating effect on women. His eyes sparkled with good humor and interest in whomever he was talking with at the moment. The fact that it was now she on whom attention was riveted quite took her breath away.

It was Cameron who escorted her into the dining room and leaned down to whisper, "My mother has designated me your official escort while you're at Montclair. So shall I have the pleasure of your company on a grand tour of the place tomorrow?"

"I should like that." Lorabeth managed to sound casually more interested in the promised view than in her escort.

"Tomorrow morning, then. The earlier the better. Or are you a 'slugabed'?"

"I'm used to getting up quite early," Lorabeth replied truthfully. She stopped short of explaining that it was the charity students' job to trot down to the school kitchens in the morning in order to fill the water pitchers for the sculleries to carry up to the paying students' rooms.

"Fine—right after breakfast," Cam confirmed.

Lorabeth could scarcely sleep that night, despite the soft embrace of the feather bed. The evening breeze scented with the perfume of a hundred varieties of flowers, drifted, like a caress, through her bedroom window from the gardens below. When at last she slept, her dreams were of Cameron.

Awake before dawn, Lorabeth rose and dressed in the riding habit Aunt Noramary had lent her the night before. She seated herself by the bedroom window to watch for Cameron.

As was her custom every morning, she took up her little Bible to read a few verses, seeking protection and guidance for the day ahead.

She felt more distracted than usual. The thought of spending time alone with Cameron both excited and troubled her. Was it wrong to feel so attracted to her handsome cousin?

Before she found the answer she was seeking, she saw him riding up from the stables on a chestnut horse nearly the color of his own hair, with a dappled-gray horse on a lead trotting alongside.

Halting under her window, Cam looked up and seeing her, smiled and brought his hand to his forehead in a salute. Lorabeth gave an answering wave, turned, ran across the room, and flew down the winding staircase, her boot-shod feet barely touching the steps.

Cameron's pride in his land was evident as they rode over the Montrose fields, along woodland paths that bordered the river at the edge of the property.

"Well, what do you think of Montclair?" Cameron asked at length, breaking a long silence between them.

"It's so—huge! All these acres and acres!" Lorabeth searched for words. "England is such a small country. Even the manor houses are not so impressive. It's a bit overwhelming, I must say."

"The original King's Grant to my great-grand-father and his brother was two thousand acres. Each of them planned to build a house on his portion; raise tobacco, corn, money crops, as well as food— each plantation to be self-sufficient. But when his brother died suddenly, without marrying or devel-oping his land, my grandfather sold parcels. The Cameron family bought some adjoining acreage, and now the Montrose property is only about fifteen hundred acres."

"*Only* fifteen hundred acres!" echoed Lorabeth. "My goodness!"

Cameron laughed at her amazement. "Virginians think big."

In front of a pasture Cam dismounted and helped Lorabeth down. Leaning on the top rail of a white board fence, they viewed a peaceful scene. Mares were grazing contentedly in the sweet grass, their frisky colts gamboling nearby. After a few minutes, Lorabeth and Cameron walked their horses back to the stables and turned them over to the grooms, then started back toward the house.

"There's so much more to see," Cameron said. "Much more I'd like to show you." He opened the gate that led to the garden Lorabeth could see from her bedroom window.

It was a perfect replica of many of the old-fashioned gardens in England—fragrant with roses, miniature apple trees, borders of iris, daffodils, and grape hyacinths.

"This spot is Mother's pride and joy." Cameron said, leading the way along the winding flagstone paths.

"It's very like a formal English garden," Lorabeth commented.

"She meant it to be. My mother loves all things English." Cameron paused and regarded Lorabeth curiously. "That still seems strange to me, you know. You, growing up on the other side of the ocean; I, never knowing you—"

Just then Noramary, carrying a reed basket overflowing with fresh-cut roses, came round the hedge.

"We're just admiring your garden, Aunt Noramary," Lorabeth said.

"It is lovely just now, isn't it? Everything is at its peak—the roses especially." She picked one, still sparkling with dew, and handed it to Lorabeth, with a smile.

Noramary smiled. "You look like a rose yourself, Lorabeth, straight out of an English garden."

Then, with a wave of her hand, Noramary turned down one of the paths and disappeared from view.

Cameron and Lorabeth strolled on, stepping onto the lawn, green and smooth as velvet and shaded by poplars, maples, and tulip trees, bordered by flowering bushes, extended on through a meadow as far as the eye could see to a sparkling ribbon of light, where the sun kissed the river.

With unspoken assent, they walked some distance farther from the house until the river was in full view.

Cameron took off his jacket and placed it on the grass for Lorabeth to sit on. Lifting her riding skirt, she sank down gracefully. She removed the tricorne hat and loosened the ribbon that bound her thick curls.

Observing the shimmering, sunlit surface, Lorabeth murmured, "What a lovely view."

"*Mine* certainly is!" Cameron said, who was, instead, admiring her delicate profile.

She turned to him with sweet surprise,

amazed that he would speak so openly. She echoed his thought, *And so is mine,* looking at Cam's chiseled features, the thick wavy hair, the generous mouth, his skin, tanned and glowing.

Cameron rushed on impulsively. "You know, I wish I'd thought to say what my mother said . . . about your looking so . . . like an English rose. I'm afraid she bested me that time, but then you've probably been told hundreds of times that you are"—his voice dropped—"quite beautiful."

As he continued to regard her, Lorabeth felt a tingling breathlessness. She was stunned by the impact of Cameron's words, yet she could not turn away from his intense gaze.

Almost in spite of herself, Lorabeth asked softly, "What are you thinking?"

"I was thinking that if you'd never come to Virginia, I might never have met you."

There seemed to be no answer for that. A long moment passed before Cameron spoke again.

"I never imagined there was someone like you."

"But—we hardly know each other . . . ," she protested.

"That's true, and yet in another way I feel we've known each other from the beginning of time. Don't you? As if we'd met somewhere, sometime before?"

A responsive emotion swept through Lorabeth at his words. So he had felt it, too!—Lorabeth felt a melting, sweet sensation, a tender yearning, a longing to hold and be held. She had never felt like this before, and yet she recognized it as old as humankind and as eternal.

Lorabeth stared at Cameron, transfixed. Something she could neither name nor understand was spinning so fast within her. What was happening? To both of them! She saw what she was experiencing reflected in Cameron's eyes.

"Why didn't you come to Virginia before I— before this?" he frowned. "After all, your mother was a widow. There was no real reason for her to stay in England, was there, with all her family here in Virginia?" Scowling, he pulled viciously at the blades of grass. "Even so, I guess it wouldn't have made any difference. . . ."

Whatever more might have been said was abruptly interrupted by a shout from across the meadow. Cameron got to his feet and turned to see a little black boy running toward them.

"Marse Cam'run!" he was calling as he ran. By the time the boy reached them, he was panting. "Mistress done sent me to fetch you. Axes that you come back to de house right now. Company here. Mistress Draper and Miss Malinda. They all waitin' fo' you, suh."

"Blast!" Cameron muttered under his breath. "All right, Matt, I'll be up presently."

Turning to Lorabeth, he said, "I guess we'd best go." He held out his hands to her, she placed hers in them, and he helped her to her feet.

"Is there some way I can get into the house and slip upstairs to make myself presentable before meeting your guests?" Lorabeth asked, brushing off her skirt.

Cameron glanced at her, started to say something, then pressed his lips together firmly.

"Yes, we'll go in around the kitchen garden. Then you can go up the back staircase to the second floor and to your room."

They walked the rest of the way in silence. Both felt there was so much to say, so much left unspoken, and yet, perhaps, better not said at all.

Chapter 6

Lorabeth reached the guest bedroom unde-
tected. Breathless from running, she leaned against
the door for a few minutes until she could breathe
easily again.

Feeling flushed, she poured some water from
the pitcher into the bowl and splashed her face
several times. Still she felt the heat rise into her
cheeks, remembering some of the unsettling
things Cameron had said to her. And her own

response—so immediate, so spontaneous, so unexpected! And yet—almost from the first—she had sensed something between them. . . .

Cameron's words came back to her as she stood patting her face with a linen towel. Had he meant them? And if he had, to what purpose? They were cousins. He was engaged—engaged to the very girl who was downstairs waiting for him at this moment and whom Lorabeth herself was about to meet. Would she share Aunt Laura's opinion of Malinda Draper? A minx who did not deserve Cameron?

Both dreading the encounter and anticipating it with perverse curiosity, Lorabeth proceeded to get dressed. For the first time in her life she was faced with the decision of which of several pretty dresses to wear. One by one she removed them from the armoire and, standing in front of the full-length mirror, held each of them against herself, studying the effect.

At length she chose a muslin sprigged with blue cornflowers, threaded with eyelet lace, and frilled with ruffles at the square neck and elbows. She brushed back her hair and tied it with a blue ribbon at the nape of her neck, letting the curls bunch in ringlets. Then she surveyed her reflection.

Against the backdrop of the luxurious bedroom, beautifully appointed in rosewood furnishings and damask bed hangings, with a soft flowered rug beneath her feet, the girl in the mirror seemed almost a stranger to Lorabeth. It was as if she now moved in a dream world that had no substance. Cameron, she reminded herself, was part of that world.

No matter what undercurrent of feeling had passed between them, nor what had been said this afternoon, the entire episode must be put away from her waking thoughts as one puts away a dream upon awakening.

With a sigh that was almost a shudder, Lorabeth turned from the glass and opened the bedroom door to the hall. She paused at the curve of the balcony. From there, she could see through the half-opened louvered doors into the drawing room beyond.

Cameron was standing, hands clasped behind him, in front of the sofa. His lean, broad-shouldered figure blocked the view of the woman to whom he was speaking, but Lorabeth glimpsed the ruffle of a hoop skirt. She heard the murmur of conversation, the tinkle of soft laughter. Placing one hand on the bannister she took a deep breath and started down the stairs.

Crossing the hall, Lorabeth came to the threshold of the drawing room. Aunt Noramary, beautiful in a French muslin dress embroidered with tiny red rosebuds, saw her and immediately came over to her. Lorabeth noticed her ruby brooch and matching earrings. These must be the same ones she was wearing in the portrait that hung on the stair landing. It had been painted during the first year she lived at Montclair. How little her aunt had changed in more than twenty years!

"How sweet you look, my dear," Noramary said, squeezing her arm. "Come, I want to introduce you to our guests."

Lorabeth's eyes moved past her aunt to the sofa where Cameron stood. Their glances touched briefly before she saw the dainty, doll-like creature, together with a plump, petulantly pretty woman. *Malinda Draper,* Lorabeth thought, and her "formidable mama."

As Noramary made the introductions, Lorabeth noticed that Malinda's china-blue eyes narrowed slightly.

"So! You're Cam's English cousin! How very odd that you should suddenly appear when nobody knew you were coming!" she said artlessly as she carefully measured Lorabeth, taking in the slender, graceful carriage, the rose and cream damask complexion—the sweet curve of the mouth. Nor did she miss the charming dimple nor the dark eyes with sweeping lashes.

After this unnerving scrutiny, Malinda turned away and began chatting animatedly to the group at large, her hand touching Cameron's arm frequently.

Lorabeth observed that it was not at all unusual

for the mistress of Montclair to entertain on an impromptu basis. That evening sixteen extra guests, including the Drapers, gathered around the dining table. As the guest of honor Lorabeth was seated to the right of Duncan Montrose. Far down the table, at his mother's left hand, sat Cameron, across from Malinda.

It was not until after dinner when the gentlemen had joined the ladies in the drawing room that Noramary suggested perhaps the younger members of the company might like to go into the parlor while some of the others settled for an evening of cards.

Servants were lighting candles at the small game tables, and the group of young folk, which included Bracken Cameron and Blakely Ashford, who had come from Cameron Hall earlier, drifted together across the hall.

"Cards bore me! I can never seem to remember what has been played!" announced Malinda, as if it were a virtue.

"Someone as pretty as you needn't bother about such weighty problems," Bracken Cameron said flatteringly but with a mischievous sparkle in his dark eyes.

"Let's play charades," she suggested, making a little pirouette in the middle of the room that sent her wide skirts spinning, her curls dancing, and her unfurled fan fluttering. Every young man in sight seemed charmed by the effect, and

Lorabeth suspected that was just the intent.

"I'm far too gastronomically overindulged for that," said Bracken languidly, sitting down on one of the wing chairs and stretching his long legs out in front of him.

"The exercise will do you good!" she retorted flippantly, affecting a pout.

Bracken groaned and, speaking in a dramatic tone, demanded sternly, *"Et tu, Brute?"*

"That's an idea—how about a game of 'Quotes'?" Cameron suggested. "That doesn't take much energy."

With a little flounce, Malinda seated herself on the smaller of two sofas, patting the pillow beside her for Cameron to join her.

"I'll begin," said Cameron, accepting the seat beside her. Then, turning to Lorabeth, he explained. "Someone recites a familiar quotation, and the next person must name it, supply an ending, or top it with another—"

"Oh, that's much too hard!" Malinda protested.

"Of course it isn't! You've played it before. . . ." Cam seemed a bit annoyed with her. But there was no edge in his voice as he asked Lorabeth, "Is this a game that is known in England?"

"No, but it sounds like fun. . . .I should like to try."

Taking Bracken's off-hand comment as his cue, Cameron pointed at the young man lounging in the chair and scoffingly quoted, "Even such a man, so faint, so spiritless, so dull, so dead in look, so woebegone—"

Bracken rose immediately to his own defense. "Shakespeare, *Henry IV*, Part II," he shouted, then laughingly countered. "Try this one—

> In all thy humors, whether grave or mellow,
> Thou'rt such a testy, touchy, pleasant fellow,
> Hast so much wit and mirth and spleen about thee
> There is no living with thee nor without thee."

Cameron frowned, and Lorabeth offered tentatively, "Addison?"

Bracken leapt to his feet, gave her a sweeping bow. "Right, dear lady. Now, your turn."

Lorabeth pondered a minute, then quoted, "If I had been present at the creation, I would have given some useful hints for the better arrangement of the Universe. . . ."

"Come now, Lorabeth. That's too obtuse," scowled Cameron.

"And even heretical, wouldn't you say?" teased Bracken.

General laughter. "Give us something simpler," begged Blakely.

She put her chin upon her hand as if in deep thought. Then: "I must be cruel only to be kind."

"Aha, Shakespeare, *Hamlet*," crowed Bracken triumphantly.

The game got off to a slow start, then grew more lively as both Blakely and Bracken, so recently back from their year at the university, began vying with each other. Quote followed quote in rapid succession. The rules included not only identifying the author of the quotation or play from which it was taken, but also contributing a line or rhyme or stanza or proverb contradicting the one just given. There was much merriment as the young people rose to the challenge.

"Wine maketh merry, but money answereth all things," quoted Bracken at his turn.

"Shakespeare, *Falstaff*?" Blakely suggested.

"Wrong!"

"Proverbs?" suggested Lorabeth.

"Right. Your turn again, m'lady," conceded Bracken with a little salute.

Dimpling and with a mischievous look in her eyes, Lorabeth tried, "*Il n'y a pas de heros pour son valet de chambre.* "

"No fair!" Cameron said indignantly. "Only English spoken here."

"*If* the lady can speak French——" Blakely came to Lorabeth's defense. "Did anyone declare a ban on another language?"

"Oh, please!" Lorabeth held up her hands in mock horror. "Please, no fighting. I'll take it back"—she made an insinuating pause—"since you are all so ignorant. . . ."

Hoots of protest and laughter followed this

remark, and Cameron said haughtily, "I know what it is: No man is a hero to his valet—of course."

"*Of course!*" the other two men chimed.

"Well, is it my turn again?"

"Cameron's."

With a dramatic flourish, he quoted, "As the great scholar and poet has said: *One* tongue is sufficient for a *woman!*"

Lorabeth put her hands on her hips as if dreadfully offended and said, "I resent that, indeed, *and*, sir, the quote is from John Milton."

"Ah, Lorabeth, you are too clever." Cameron shook his head sadly, but his eyes shone with admiration.

"Go ahead, Lorabeth," Blakely said respectfully, obviously impressed by her skill.

She thought a minute. "When in Rome, do as the Romans do, when elsewhere, live as they live elsewhere."

The tempo of the game picked up, with quotes and their sources flying back and forth like shuttlecocks, each person eager to guess the right author or to baffle the others.

Lorabeth, whose father had delighted in teaching his quick-minded daughter from his own love of the classics, was in her element. As the evening progressed, no one seemed to notice that Malinda, with her small store of knowledge of such things, had dropped out of the game.

Once, at Blakely's turn, looking directly at Lorabeth, he recited:

> "There is a lady, sweet and kind
> Was never face so pleased my mind
> I did but see her passing by
> And yet I love her till I die."

"Thomas Ford, sixteenth-century poet," Cameron responded curtly. Then he, also looking at Lorabeth, quoted:

> "Twice or thrice I love thee,
> Before I knew thy face or name."

At this, Malinda darted a quick look at Lorabeth, then at Cameron, and with a little flounce she got to her feet and gave an exaggerated yawn, half concealed behind her fan.

"Oh, for pity's sake, that's enough, Cam. Such a silly game, so childish! Come along, let's see if your mother will play for us a bit so we can dance."

"I am sure the grapes are sour," said Bracken, sotto voice.

To which Lorabeth spontaneously replied, "*Aesop's Fables*, 'The Fox and the Grapes,'" then quickly colored, aware that Bracken was criticizing Malinda for breaking up a game in which she could not keep up with the others. She was stricken, for even though she did not care for Malinda, she would never have deliberately hurt or embarrassed anyone.

With unconcealed reluctance, because he had been thoroughly enjoying the contest, Cameron got to his feet. Malinda slipped her hand possessively through his arm.

The girl was pulling Cameron away when he shrugged and said over his shoulder, "When fate summons, even monarchs must obey!"

"Dryden," retorted Bracken. "But that's no excuse, my lad: Each man is the architect of his own fate," he called after the departing couple.

They could not hear Cameron's reply, if any, and the game ended abruptly, leaving Lorabeth with the two young men.

"I suppose we should join the others in the drawing room, too," she quickly suggested, rising.

"Where did you become so learned, madam, if I may ask?" Bracken stood also and offered her his arm.

"My father was a schoolmaster, and a teacher teaches!" she said lightly.

"And what a bright pupil you must have been."

"And lovely as well." That was Blakely at her other side, extending his arm.

With a smile, Lorabeth accepted their escort into the drawing room. But beneath her smile lurked the nagging feeling that she had somehow, by her skill at the unimportant game, earned Malinda's enmity.

*   *   *

For the rest of the evening Malinda very deliberately monopolized Cam, making it impossible for him to rejoin the group. Blakely, who was totally taken with Lorabeth, seemed happy to be without competition for her attention and spent the remainder of the night at her side.

It was not until after midnight, when everyone had left and Lorabeth was in her room alone, that she found the note Cam had managed to slip into her fan case.

She held the piece of paper in shaking hands.

Meet me at the stables early in the morning. Montclair is lovely at dawn. I want to show it to you.

A quicksilver tremor slithered down her spine—a premonition of danger. Lorabeth felt caught between caution and longing.

She blew out her candle and crossed to the window, where the moon was shining in on the bare floor in dappled patterns of light. She thrust it open and leaned on the sill, savoring the sweet-scented air of the garden below.

She recalled the evening—the repartee, the sharp meeting of her mind with Cam's as they played at "Quotes," the unspoken communication that each had conveyed to the other. Could all that have been happenstance only? Or were they, in some mystical way, meant for each other?

She put cold hands to her flaming cheeks, shaken by the dawning recognition. Yet could the emotions she and Cameron had stirred in each other be any kind of meaningful love? They barely knew each other. Such things occurred only in storybooks, fantasy romances, she reminded herself. And . . . romantic love for a *cousin*? That was a forbidden kind of love—as star-crossed as Romeo and Juliet, Lorabeth thought ruefully.

As Juliet had cautioned Romeo about their sudden awakening: "It is too rash, too unadvised, too sudden. Too like the lightning, which doth cease to be, 'Ere one can say it lightens."

On the other hand, Lorabeth countered, what harm would it do to go riding together? Perhaps she was presuming something on Cameron's part that did not even exist. Why should she deprive herself of her cousin's delightful company? It was all probably her own imagination, she decided, yawning.

Chapter 7

But the next night as Lorabeth dressed to go to the Camerons' ball, she knew meeting Cam at dawn had been a mistake. She was in a state of exaggerated excitement, her head whirling with the enormity of her dilemma. Over and over every detail of what had happened between her and Cameron that morning came back to her vividly.

"I must be calm! I must," she told herself

nervously as a tap on the bedroom door and Aunt Laura's soft voice reminded her that the carriage was waiting to take them to Cameron Hall and that Grandmother Barnwell was already inside.

Picking up her lace mitts, her fan and shawl, Lorabeth glided across the room and, with her hooped skirt sliding on the polished stairway, hurried downstairs and out into the soft spring evening.

Betsy Barnwell looked at her granddaughter with approval, presuming her flushed cheeks and bright eyes were from happy anticipation of the evening ahead.

Betsy, of course, had no idea that instead of looking forward to the gala party, Lorabeth was dreading it because she did not know how she could bear seeing Cameron again after what had passed between them in the morning.

Was it too late to remedy anything? Her heart clutched as if being wrung with cold hands. Oh, how hopeless it all was!

Oblivious to the chaos in Lorabeth's heart, Betsy regarded her admiringly, thinking, *How pretty Lorabeth is. Far prettier than Winnie ever was*, she conceded rather guiltily, observing Lorabeth's exquisite profile, the rounded perfection of her small bosom, the sheen of her pale blond hair. Yes, she would be quite a sensation at the ball this evening, Betsy was sure. The blue gown, beautifully fitted through the bodice that emphasized her slender waist, with silk forget-me-nots sewn about the décolletage, ruffles of starched lace, and loops of lace banding the skirt, was a perfect complement to Lorabeth's delicate beauty, Betsy observed with satisfaction.

How badly the poor dear had needed a new wardrobe, she thought. How could Winnie have sent her off on her journey so poorly clad? Betsy frowned. *There is more to this than meets the eye,* she mused. Perhaps Winnie would explain more about Lorabeth's unexpected arrival when next she wrote—*if* she wrote. In the twenty-odd years since Winnie had eloped with that dastardly Jouquet, she had heard infrequently from her daughter. Betsy sighed. *What's done is done,* she reminded herself philosophically. *What is past repair is past tears.*

A long line of carriages already were in the drive as the Barnwells approached Cameron Hall. Elegantly gowned ladies and well-dressed gentlemen were alighting and moving up the broad stone steps of the house. The Montrose carriage took its turn in the parade.

Cameron Hall was larger and far more splendid than Montclair, Lorabeth thought, entering the many-arched front hall. Dozens of candles in crystal chandeliers glittered like diamonds. Standing to receive their guests were Judge and Mrs. Cameron, resplendent in a wide-skirted yellow satin gown; beside her stood Bracken.

Smiling broadly, he greeted Lorabeth. "Welcome to Cameron Hall. I know *someone* whose happiness will be complete now that you have finally arrived. Someone who has been watching the doorway all evening."

Lorabeth blushed, knowing he meant Blakely Ashford. But Blakely was far from her thoughts. It was Cameron she both longed, yet dreaded, to see.

In the downstairs parlor where the ladies were to leave their wraps, Lorabeth delayed as long as possible, reluctant to enter the center hall knowing Blakely would be waiting for her. Looking into one of the mirrors, Lorabeth did not see herself at all. Instead, she saw Cameron's face as he had looked that morning.

That morning, while the household still slept, Lorabeth slipped quietly downstairs and out to the stables. There she met Cam, who had the same gentle mare saddled for Lorabeth to ride.

At first they trotted companionably down the road that led from the stables. At the edge of the woods, however, Cameron took the lead, pursuing a carpeted path of pine needles through the woods where the sun was just beginning to burnish the treetops.

The sound of their horses' hooves crossing a

wooden arched bridge was all that disturbed the peace of early morning.

When they reached a clearing just beyond, Cameron reined his horse and turned in the saddle, pointing to a small house nestled deep in a circle of cedars.

"That's 'Eden Cottage,'" he told her. "It's the model for the big house. Mother named it." He smiled and shrugged. "No one knows exactly why she chose that name, except that she and Father spent the first night of their marriage there. Actually they were on their way to Montclair but were caught in a storm. A flash flood washed out the bridge . . ." He paused. "But then you should get *her* to tell you their love story."

They rode on a little farther before Cam suggested stopping beside the stream to let the horses drink. In one fluid motion he was on the ground, then hurried to Lorabeth's side and extended his hand to help her dismount.

Still holding her hand in his, he led her to a fallen log where they sat down. The woodland quiet wrapped them in a soft mantle, with only the ripple of water over rocks and an occasional birdsong to break the stillness.

It was Cameron who spoke at last. "I love you, Lorabeth," he said slowly, lifting her small hand to his lips and kissing each fingertip. "I'm not sure when or how it happened—only that it did. Maybe the first time I laid eyes on you."

Shocked by his confession as much as thrilled by his touch, Lorabeth withdrew her hand. Quickly she rose and took a few steps away from him. She could hardly breathe.

He followed instantly—his arms going around her waist, his head bending against her cheek. "I know. I know all the reasons this shouldn't have happened," he whispered. "But I don't know what to do about it, because it *has* happened."

Lorabeth's heart was pounding now. Every nerve was tingling, responding to his nearness. Yet every instinct told her she should resist him. His arms tightened, and she closed her eyes, biting back the impulsive words that sprang to her own lips.

Gently he turned her so she was facing him. They looked into each other's eyes as if for the first, or perhaps the last, time. Some bond was forged in that look that neither had felt before.

She tried to break away. Her heart fluttered in frantic warning. But before she could, he had clasped her firmly to him. His mouth was warm on hers in a kiss that was at once tender and demanding. In spite of herself, her longing overtook her caution, and she responded, winding her arms about his neck, her whole body trembling as she returned his kiss.

A lifetime of longing for love was fulfilled in

the passing of a moment! Then, her lips still feeling the warmth of his, Lorabeth drew back, staring at Cameron in disbelief. Slowly she shook her head, reached up and touched his cheek with her hand.

"This—shouldn't have happened—it cannot be. Don't you know that?"

Cameron frowned fiercely. His arms loosened about her. "You mean because of Malinda?" he demanded.

"And because . . . even more impossible. We *are,* after all, cousins."

"Cousins *do* marry," he blurted out stubbornly.

"*First* cousins?" she reproached him gently. They both knew the tragic results that had sometimes come of reckless intermarrying.

"But I don't want to think about that," Cameron said, crushing her to him. She could feel every muscle in his body stiffening.

"I only know what I feel and I know I love you!" His words sounded as if they came through clenched teeth.

Then, still holding her with one arm, he tilted her chin with his other hand and searched her face with an almost desperate yearning. For an endless moment they looked into each other's eyes, asking the same question, receiving the same answer. The next thing Lorabeth felt was Cam's kiss, infinitely sweet and tender. She did not resist.

Finally, with great effort, she pulled out of his arms.

"We'd better be getting back now," she said shakily.

"I know," Cameron sighed. "Lorabeth, maybe I shouldn't have said anything. But . . . I knew . . . I thought you felt the same and . . ."

He held her horse's bridle while she mounted, then stood looking up at her.

"No matter what, I can't take back the words. I *do* love you, Lorabeth, cousin or not."

She looked away from those searching eyes, because she could not bear to see what he could not hide. She felt the sting of quick tears, turned her horse and, with a light flick of her small crop, started cantering along the path back to Montclair.

Cameron caught up with her. As she tried to control her emotional reaction to the hopelessness of their situation, he reached over and took her reins, bringing both horses to a halt.

Then he jumped down from his horse, came over to her, put his hands around her waist, and lifted her out of her side-saddle and into his arms. There was no defense. Lorabeth clung to him helplessly, her emotions in turmoil.

He stood there, holding her for a long moment before she eased herself from his embrace, as loath to leave him as he was to let her go.

Finally, he helped her mount and climbed

back on his own horse. They walked the horses for a distance, as if to prolong their time together. When Montclair came into view, Lorabeth urged her mare into a canter, and they rode into the stable yard.

The stable boys led the horses away, and Lorabeth and Cameron took the path through the kitchen garden to the house. As they moved along the flagstone walkways, he bent down, snapped something from his mother's herb garden, and handed it to Lorabeth.

"There's rosemary, that's for remembrance, pray love, remember—" he whispered.

And Lorabeth whispered back, "*Hamlet* . . . Act V, Scene V."

Remember? Lorabeth blinked back tears. How could she forget? That was the real question.

"Come along, Lorabeth. You look as pretty as can be. No need for any more primping." Aunt Laura's teasing voice jolted Lorabeth back to the present. The scene in the morning woods faded abruptly as she spun around from the mirror.

"Come on, dear," Aunt Laura urged gently. "I can see poor Blakely from here, pacing the hall, eager to claim the first dance with you."

Aunt Laura was right. As soon as the women emerged into the hall, milling with groups of gaily dressed people drifting from one parlor to the other, there stood the patient Blakely, waiting.

Laura watched them go toward the sound of the lively music coming from both parlors—he, tall, fine-looking in blue satin, frothed with lace; she, small, slim, graceful, in her swinging hooped gown. *What a handsome couple they make!* She smiled to herself. And almost on top of that came the irrelevant thought, *Oh dear! Lorabeth just may break Blakely's heart.*

Now why in the world would she think such a thing, Laura asked herself. Quickly she brushed away the startling thought and went to find her mother so that she could be comfortably settled to watch the dancing.

On the dance floor, Lorabeth found herself only half-listening to Blakely's quiet conversation as they moved through the intricate steps of the first quadrille. Her eyes moved among the dancers, searching. Then, with a kind of chill, she saw the tall figure she had been looking for—and he was with Malinda.

At the sight of them together, Lorabeth felt a stab of resentment so violent she was shaken by its force. If it had not been clear to her before what she felt for Cameron, she understood now. For if Lorabeth had never known love until Cameron, she had never known jealousy until Malinda.

Quickly she prayed for forgiveness. To be fair, Malinda *was* enchanting. It was easy to see why any man—even Cameron—might be bewitched by her pert manner, her coquettishness, the creamy skin, flirtatious, long-lashed blue eyes.

It was mean and shallow and wicked of her to be envious, Lorabeth scolded herself. She must forget this morning's madness, the reckless way she had responded to Cameron's kisses. He was betrothed to Malinda, a commitment almost as binding as marriage. Besides, he was her cousin. There was no future for them.

But all her arguments and resolutions vanished in a second when the music ended and suddenly Cameron, handsome in a claret-satin coat and lace jabot, stood in front of her, bowing and requesting the honor of the next dance.

As she looked up at him, Lorabeth saw her own surge of joy mirrored in his eyes. Almost dizzy with irrational happiness, she put her hand in his and let him lead her onto the dance floor.

Chapter 8

The carriage carrying Lorabeth and Aunt Laura back to Williamsburg rumbled over rutted country roads. Grandmother Betsy had returned home the morning after the Camerons' ball, but Noramary had prevailed upon the others to remain for a few days longer.

Preoccupied and pensive, Lorabeth stared out the window as each mile took her farther and farther from Montclair and Cameron. *A safe distance,* she thought ironically. As if any place on earth would be safe from thoughts of Cameron now! She allowed herself the luxury of thinking about him. What harm was there in that, since nothing could come of it?

He must have realized it, too. For after the ball, he had made it a point to be away from the house much of the time Lorabeth remained at Montclair. It was as if they had made a mutual decision, an unspoken pact, that in the future they must avoid each other entirely.

The presence of almost constant company at Montclair helped to ease the pain. Malinda and her mother, for instance, made frequent visits while Lorabeth and her aunt were there. And Blakely, who was still the Camerons' houseguest, rode over every day to call on Lorabeth.

Maybe it was easier that way. Lorabeth could not imagine another intense encounter with Cameron. All she knew was they must be careful from now on. What they felt for each other might become too obvious, even to the casual observer. They must learn somehow to live with the reality of what could never be. And with the families so close, that would be the most difficult task of all.

"We must celebrate your birthday here!" Noramary had said as she kissed Lorabeth good-bye. "I've already discussed it with Aunt Betsy and she has agreed. September is such a lovely month—not so hot as summer, and not yet cold."

Cameron was nowhere in sight that morning when they left. Perhaps he had not dared to say his farewell in front of everyone.

Up to the last minute, she had been conscious of her tension—a mixed dread and longing for him to appear. But he didn't, and she got into the carriage without seeing him again.

It is for the best, she decided wearily, leaning her head back upon the velvet upholstery.

Although they reached Williamsburg long after dark, a light supper had been prepared to welcome the travelers home. Aunt Laura said some tea was all she wanted and, pleading a slight headache and fatigue, said good night, took her cup, and went straight up to bed.

Lorabeth, however, felt very hungry and followed her grandmother into the small parlor where a table set with snowy linen held a dish of fruit, a plate of sandwiches, lemon pound cake, and a silver pot of tea.

Lorabeth chatted cheerfully about the visitors and events that had taken place at Montclair after her grandmother's return to Williamsburg. She was conscious, however, of a peculiar lack of response on Betsy's part. When she had brushed the crumbs of her second piece of cake into her napkin and wiped her fingers carefully, she looked up to see Betsy regarding her speculatively. Then her grandmother got up, settled herself in her favorite wingchair, and motioned Lorabeth to sit on the love seat facing her.

"Lorabeth, my dear, I think it is time we had a nice talk," her grandmother began gently. As she spoke she picked up an envelope from the little piecrust table beside her and tapped the edge of it against her teeth thoughtfully.

Lorabeth felt a stirring of apprehension as her grandmother fixed her with a sharp, inquiring look.

"I received a letter from your mother, my dear, and it has raised a number of questions. I am sure you must be aware of some of them." She paused significantly. "Life is full of surprises, as I surely know from my own experiences, but I must admit this comes as quite a shock."

Under her Grandmother Barnwell's unrelenting gaze, Lorabeth felt her knees begin to shake. She took the place on the love seat Betsy had indicated, and clasped her hands tightly in her lap.

"In this letter your mother says you are—to quote her—a 'runaway.' Is that true? Did you leave England without her knowedge? And is there a gentleman to whom a great deal of explanation is in order?"

"Oh, Grandmother!" Lorabeth said in dismay. There was a long pause, then she blurted out, "Yes! It is all true! Oh Grandmother, I'm so sorry. I should have told you. I was going to . . . I didn't think Mama would catch up with me this soon or that a letter could arrive before I had a chance . . ." Lorabeth's voice broke .

She buried her head in both hands for a moment, then lifted it bravely. "You see, without my consent Mama arranged an engagement. Not that she needed my consent, of course, but at least, one should be fond of—or at least feel something less than aversion for—the person one is supposed to marry, shouldn't one?

"Oh, it's all such a muddle! I don't know whether or not I can explain, or if you could possibly understand—"

"Well, do try, dear, . . . and *I* shall try to understand," Betsy said, with a slight twitching of her lips.

"Ever since Father died, or even before that, I suppose, Mama kept telling me that with my looks and my brains I should be able to—to use her words—make a fine catch. Over and over she would say how very important it was to make a good marriage."

Betsy controlled an impulse to comment in view of Winnifred's own disastrous choice. Lorabeth's next words, however, assured Betsy that her daughter had learned something in the years of her exile since her youthful escapade.

"I know it was wrong to resent her constant nagging. Mama meant it for my own good! She doesn't want me to end up as she did . . . first, the widow of a penniless n'er-do-well, then, of an impoverished schoolmaster. That is why she went to such trouble to bring me up as a lady, with all the refinement and manners and accomplishments you instilled in her.

"And poor Father—he insisted on educating me as well. He kept saying he could not let a bright mind go fallow. So I really don't fit in anywhere in England, where everything depends so much on one's family background. The only other option was becoming a governess. . . .And Mama insisted my prospects for marriage were such that I would never have to resort to caring for someone else's children."

At this point Lorabeth jumped to her feet and, unconsciously wringing her small hands, began pacing in front of her grandmother as she went on with her explanation.

"When I returned to school last fall after the summer holiday, I knew things were becoming difficult at home. The house we lived in belonged to the school and would have to be given up when the new headmaster arrived to take over Father's position. We had been allowed to remain there only because they had not yet secured someone approved by their Board.

"I had been promised a teaching position when I completed my education, so we felt it was best for me to continue there, since I got my tuition and board by helping in the lower forms and tutoring some of the slower pupils.

"But just before the Christmas holidays, I got a letter from Mama, declaring that she believed she had made an arrangement that would benefit us both and secure our future. I could not have imagined what it was, but was pleased that Mama was not so melancholy and worried as before.

"However, what she had arranged was for me to marry—or at least to accept as a serious suitor— Mr. Horace Merriman."

Here Lorabeth paused dramatically, waiting for some reaction from her grandmother. When none was forthcoming, she went on in a trembling voice.

"I cannot tell you how unhappy this made me, Grandmother. I didn't want to marry. Certainly not someone I couldn't even remember having ever seen. But Mama said it was all but settled—that she had invited Mr. Merriman to have tea with us on my first day home. She reminded me of our situation and hoped I would take every means to make a good impression. She told me that he was a prosperous merchant with a lovely home and other property, that he had been a widower for a number of years and was eager to marry again. She presented all the reasons, all the advantages of such a marriage. But, Grandmother, I honestly think the greatest advantage was that I would be off her hands! And that's what I did, didn't I? I took myself off her hands!

"Well, to make a long tale brief . . . I came home on holiday. Such a fuss, such preparations, and then—when I met Mr. Merriman . . . Well, Grandmother, he was way past forty and totally bald. His wig kept slipping and I could see the pink scalp underneath . . . and he had a paunch so that his waistcoat buttons were gaping . . . and oh, it was dreadful."

Here Lorabeth whirled about and flung out her hands despairingly. "Grandmother, he talked about his house, and I could see from what he said that I would have to move right in and live in that house, just as it was, with all his first wife's things, her furniture and her pictures and her china. . . .Well I just couldn't do it! I simply couldn't. And so I refused his suit. There was the most awful scene. And Mama went to bed with a sick headache, saying I was an ungrateful girl. She was still hardly speaking to me when I returned to school before the holiday was up."

Lorabeth, looking distressed, sighed deeply before continuing. "Mama barely wrote to me the next few months while I was still at school, after I wrote the note to Mr. Merriman officially refusing his proposal.

"Well, sometime later Mama took the position of housekeeper with the Fairchilds, a wealthy family of Kent. She was given her own suite of rooms, luxuriously furnished, and ran the household for Squire Fairchild, who had been a widower for years and was in ill health. At last Mama had what she had never been able to afford. But when I came home for the summer at the end of the term, another conflict arose between us. It came in the person of Willie Fairchild, a distant relative of the Squire's and quite obnoxious—in my opinion. To make matters worse, this person, Willie Fairchild, made himself quite a nuisance. But Mama was terribly impressed by his family background. She kept reminding me of what lay ahead of me unless I was sensible and accepted him! But, Grandmother, he was foppish. I know that sounds harsh, but after all, I am, by my father's own words, an intelligent person capable of a great deal of understanding and comprehension, and the thought of spending the rest of my life with such a silly person was more than I could bear.

"Mama threw a dreadful fit. She reminded me that she was still young herself, and attractive, with many admirers of her own. That she could have married again many times, but that she had to take care of me until I was safely married. She demanded I accept Willie."

Her slender shoulders seemed to slump, and Lorabeth shook her head sadly. "I returned to school in despair. I was so torn between duty to my mother and my own feelings.

"Truly, Grandmother, I believe Providence provided me an escape. I had become friends with one of the students, Dora Carrington, an orphaned heiress, who was often lonely. We spent much time together. She confided that her dead parents' lawyer had arranged for her to leave England and make her home with relatives she had never met on a sugar plantation in the West Indies. She hated the idea and did not want to go, because she was in love with a fine young man. She begged me to help her elope with him. Naturally I sympathized with her situation.

"Now, Grandmother, you may say two wrongs don't make a right, but we were both desperate! We formed a plan for our mutual benefit. Since her passage and ticket had already been bought, and the school notified of her departure, I volunteered to accompany her and see her safely on board ship. Instead, her young man met her and off they went, I pray, to live happily ever after. She had given me leave to exchange her ticket to Jamaica for passage on an American ship coming to Virginia. I wrote a letter to Mama that would reach her after the ship sailed."

Here, Lorabeth's voice broke, and the tears that had been hovering, spilled over and rolled down her cheeks unchecked.

"I know you will think I was deceitful and disobedient to do what I did, Grandmother. And I am truly sorry to have hurt Mama or offended you. But can you understand at all how I could not bring myself to marry someone I hardly knew . . . and could never love?"

Her grandmother pursed her lips and tapped the edge of the envelope against the polished tabletop thoughtfully.

"If it's true that your mother's main ambition is to see you married to a man of property and wealth . . . it would not matter precisely who the man was? Am I correct? Therefore, if we had someone in mind, equally well endowed, should she not be as pleased? In other words, we can—as the saying goes—catch two birds with one net, eh? Never fret, my dear. I shall take care of this. No need to worry your poor little head any longer. If your mother's price is money . . . then we shall *ransom* you!"

"*Ransom me?*" Lorabeth looked puzzled, but a flicker of hope rose within her. "How?" she asked.

"I hear, from three reliable sources—Laura, Noramary, and Jacqueline Cameron—that young Blakely Ashford is, to coin a phrase, "sick with love' for you, dear child. A finer young man of more distinguished family would be hard to find. He would meet every requirement of your mother's and more. In fact, as his wife, you would be one of the wealthiest young women in Virginia. He stands to inherit a fortune from both parents, as well as being independently wealthy.

"As you can see, he is good-looking, nice mannered, of pleasant personality, and no breath of scandal has ever touched him. I think, as a comparative match, this Willie Fairchild might run a poor second. What say you, Lorabeth? Could you find it in your heart to look kindly on young Ashford's proposal?"

Lorabeth swallowed hard. She knew there was no place in her heart for any man since she had met and fallen hopelessly in love with Cameron. *Hopelessly.* Yes, that was the word for it.

Her grandmother, seeing her hesitation, prodded gently, "The alternative, of course, is what your mother suggests—that we put you on the next ship sailing for England . . . and into the waiting arms of Willie Fairchild," she added, with a tinge of irony.

"Oh, no, Grandmother! I do want to stay in Virginia," Lorabeth protested.

"Well, then, shall I make Blakely aware that we look upon his suit favorably? By the subtlest of means . . ."

Betsy let the thought dangle tentatively as she

watched her granddaughter's reaction to the idea.

Lorabeth's face in the firelight, eyes bright with tears, the red lips parted as if ready to answer, touched her grandmother's heart. What a child this lovely young woman still was. A child in need of comfort and advice and help.

Heavy-hearted, Lorabeth hesitated only a minute longer, then sighed and said, "Yes, Grandmother . . . I suppose that is what I must do."

"Then leave everything to me, my dear. We shall work out the best possible solution to this problem. I shall write your mother that what we have in mind is beyond her own dreams for you."

She patted the soft cheek and spoke reassuringly. "Now run along to bed. You are worn out. And you need your beauty sleep."

Betsy Barnwell gazed after the small, slim figure of Lorabeth and shook her head slightly. Well, there was nothing to do but to figure some way out of it. Goodness knows she'd had enough experience at such things. And there was no way that she was going to let that sweet young thing go back to her grasping, ambitious mother, even if Winnie *was* her own daughter!

Lorabeth lay long awake in the canopy bed in which her mother had slept as a girl and faced, alone in the dark, the harshest reality yet encountered in her short life.

She was caught in a web not of her own making. She tried to have compassion for her mother, who, also, had had to face harsh realities alone. All her life Lorabeth had heard how Winnie had been abandoned by the irresponsible Jouquet, left alone until taken in by the headmaster of the school where the Frenchman had taught before eloping with one of the wealthy pupils. When the headmaster's young and delicate wife died, Winnie had married the widower, Lorabeth's father. As Lorabeth grew up, she realized theirs had not been a marriage of love, but of convenience, for there could not have been two more unlikely partners. Her gentle, bookish father; her snappish, discontented mother. Lorabeth understood how her experiences might have embittered her mother. Still, she could not allow herself to be forced by circumstances into a loveless marriage.

Blakely was kind, gentle, handsome, intelligent—everything any sensible girl could want in a husband. It would be easy to learn to love him—*if* she had never met Cameron.

To think that less than a month ago she had not even known Cameron Montrose existed. Now he filled her world. His face, his voice, the way he moved and smiled, consumed her waking thoughts and her dreams at night! Without him her world would be empty. But they both knew their love was impossible.

If she returned to England, she would likely

never see him again. And that would be even worse. One was dying by inches; the other, sudden death. Lorabeth pulled the quilt over her head and wept the bitterest, loneliest tears of her lifetime.

Chapter 9

The September afternoon was as warm as June in the Barnwells' back garden. Only the scarlet tinge on the gold maple leaves and the brisk breeze causing the shaggy purple asters and orange wall flowers to dance, hinted of autumn.

Standing at her parlor window, Betsy observed with satisfaction the two young people strolling along the brick paths. Lorabeth, dainty in pink muslin, the lacy film of fichu outlining delicately the gentle roundness of her bosom, chatted with Blakely, who was all attentiveness.

An indulgent smile played around Betsy's mouth. Young Ashford was certainly enamored of her charming granddaughter, she sighed happily. And what more could any young girl want in a suitor? Courteous, considerate, handsome, with manners and wealth besides. Winnie could not have arranged a better match herself, Betsy thought smugly. Yes, Blakely's ardent courtship of Lorabeth had fit perfectly into her own plans. It had been a wise decision to "ransom" Lorabeth by promising Winnie if she allowed the girl to remain in Virginia that she was sure to make an advantageous marriage. Indeed, things could not be progressing more smoothly.

Winnie, however, had not accepted defeat gracefully. Betsy recalled with some indignation the sharply worded reply from Lorabeth's mother. At the time, Betsy had simply dismissed it with a shrug, as a display of Winnie's predictable temper. She had always been a difficult child—the only one of her children to rebel openly—and had grown into an equally difficult woman. It was almost as if Winnie resented Lorabeth's opportunity to marry an American and live in Virginia! Well, she had thrown away her own chances by her youthful folly. Now she must reap what she had sown, Betsy thought grimly.

In the garden, quite unaware of the grandmotherly surveillance, Lorabeth halted for a moment to pluck some of the flowers and make them into a nosegay. Blakely said something in a low tone of voice and, as she turned toward him to hear him better, the rose-colored ribbon that bound her curls came loose and her long, silky hair fell in a cascade over her shoulders.

Blakely caught the ribbon and, as Lorabeth reached for it, he took her hand instead, lifted it to his lips, then held it, winding the ribbon around her third finger, left hand, as if measuring it.

They stood gazing at each other for a long moment. Betsy, witnessing the pretty little scene, turned away. In her romantic heart she felt sure Blakely was about to make the hoped-for proposal.

At supper Lorabeth seemed quietly thoughtful. Betsy kept waiting for Lorabeth's announcement, for certainly the girl knew how anxious her grandmother was to know if her well-laid plans had come to fruition. But Lorabeth seemed almost pensive.

It was her aunt who inadvertently sensed Lorabeth's unusual introspectiveness and asked gently, "Are you well, dear? You don't seem quite yourself this evening."

"It's been a busy summer," Betsy interjected provocatively. "So many callers, so many parties, so much visiting back and forth." She paused significantly. It was, after all, Blakely who had been the most frequent "caller," Lorabeth's faithful escort to rounds of parties and fêtes, as well as Sunday services. But Lorabeth did not take the cue. So then Betsy said briskly, "It's probably this long hot spell. You know, Laura, Lorabeth isn't used to the Virginia climate yet. She does look a bit pale. Perhaps some sage tea would help."

Lorabeth meekly submitted to the prescribed treatment—sipping the strong, spicy beverage under her aunt's concerned supervision. Only *she* knew there was nothing wrong with her strange apathy, the result of what had taken place in the garden that afternoon.

All summer she had accepted the flattering attention of this very personable young man as he pursued the approved pattern of courtship. She had grown very fond of Blakely, who was delightful company, amusing, affable, and respectfully affectionate. He had wooed her by every traditional means—with flowers, poetry, confections of all kinds, small gifts—all within the acceptable, rigid code of what a young gentleman should offer and what a young lady could receive.

Without a doubt she knew the fairly obvious ploy he had chosen, wrapping her finger with the ribbon, had implied his next gift would be a betrothal ring.

Ah, well, Lorabeth sighed. It was exactly what Grandmother had wanted, the precise solution to her prickly problem—and yet—if only she could forget Cameron Montrose, then she could, perhaps, be content.

As they left the dining room, while crossing the hall into the small parlor, Betsy could not contain her curiosity any longer. She slipped her arm through Lorabeth's and asked in a confidential tone, "So, did young Ashford finally find the nerve to propose?"

Taken by surprise, not knowing her grandmother had witnessed the intimate little tableau in the garden, Lorabeth answered, "Why, yes, Grandmother, this very afternoon. He asked if I cared enough for him to speak to his parents about an engagement before approaching you for permission."

"How splendid!" Betsy exclaimed. "The announcement could be made at your birthday ball at Montclair." She gave Lorabeth's arm an excited little squeeze. "Didn't I tell you, my dear, that we would 'ransom' you from that unhappy situation at home? Now there's no more cause for worry." She gave Lorabeth a reassuring pat. "Did you hear that, Laura? Lorabeth has some very interesting news. It looks like a wedding is in the offing!"

Laura gave Lorabeth a hug. "Now we can be sure you will remain in Virginia! I've so dreaded the thought of losing you on the chance that your mother would insist on your return to England. Now we can all be happy."

Happy? Lorabeth wished she could share her aunt's and grandmother's jubilance. They began chatting about what must be done about her trousseau as if the matter were already settled.

While they seated themselves and began a discussion of fabrics, choice of trim and lace, Lorabeth wandered into the music room adjoining the small parlor and sat down at the harpsichord. Her fingers ran idly over the keyboard while her mind was filled with errant thoughts of Cameron.

If it had been possible to avoid him, it might have been easier. But at every one of the summer parties, fêtes, and picnics, they had met. He was, of course, always in attendance with Malinda and she, in the company of Blakely.

"That's a nice idea, my dear. Play something light and spritely," her grandmother called.

The music soothed the aching in her heart. She had not realized, even though she knew their paths were bound to cross just as Cameron had predicted, that each time it would be like a knife thrust in her breast. If only . . .

Lorabeth had been playing for perhaps a half hour when suddenly the front door burst open and, caught by the wind, slammed sharply against the wall. Grandmother and Aunt Laura jumped, and Lorabeth abruptly stopped her playing. There in the doorway stood Cameron.

"Sorry to startle you, Auntie B.," he said, grinning, as his eyes roamed the room seeking Lorabeth.

When they found her at the harpsichord, they feasted on her like a starving man. Then he reluctantly crossed the room to focus on Betsy and to explain his unexpected appearance.

"I came into Williamsburg this morning on plantation business for my father, and things took longer to conclude than I expected. It's now too late to start back for Montclair. May I stay the night?"

Lorabeth, meanwhile, tried to still her trembling hands, quiet her pounding heart. It was as if by her thoughts of him, she had brought him here.

Cameron's eyes once again sought Lorabeth, his voice drifting off as if entranced by the picture she made, her face softly lighted by the candles in the sconces on either side of the music rack.

Betsy, who never missed a thing, saw the look and felt a twinge of apprehension. She also noticed how Lorabeth's face had flushed at his glance, acknowledging his presence with a sweet, wistful expression.

"Do go on playing, Lorabeth," he commanded. "Don't let me interrupt a concert. I'm a real connoisseur of music, am I not, Aunt Laura?" He gave a brittle laugh. "Never could learn how to read notes, no matter how hard you tried to teach me, could I? So, Lorabeth, if you make a mistake, I'll never know the difference."

"Lorabeth plays beautifully," Aunt Laura protested.

"I'll come turn the pages for you," offered Cameron, going over to the harpsichord.

Betsy saw Lorabeth's face lifted like a flower to the sun as her tall cousin came over to stand beside her. Her perceptive eyes noted the intimate smile that passed between them, and an inner warning sounded in her mind, chilling her with its truth.

So that's the way the land lies! Well, I must do something about it, right away, before a worse disaster than Lorabeth being sent back to England occurs.

Quickly gathering her wits, she addressed Cameron directly. "Of course, dear boy, you know you're always welcome. In fact, you're just in time to hear the news. We're planning Lorabeth's birthday ball, which is, as you know, to be held at Montclair. And now we've learned that something else may be the cause of even greater celebration—Lorabeth's engagement to Blakely Ashford! What better time to announce such a happy event than at the ball?"

Betsy's sharp eyes did not fail to detect Lorabeth's sudden pallor, the slight stiffening of Cameron's shoulders. Lorabeth's hands faltered momentarily on the keys, striking a discordant note.

These reactions were almost imperceptible. Only Betsy, her intuition sharpened by the years, would have noticed. Something had happened between them. Something strong and irrevocable, she felt sure. When? And how had it happened so quickly? But then young love was the most unreliable emotion there was. Like a will-o-the-wisp, it blew where it wandered and lighted where it would.

It was a good thing that Cameron's engagement to Malinda Draper had taken place months ago, she sighed inwardly. From what she had heard, Betsy was certain wedding preparations had already begun. Now Blakely and Lorabeth's engagement must be announced before—*before what?* Betsy demanded of herself.

Of course, engagements had been known to be broken—but not without much upheaval, gossip, even scandal, she knew too well from personal experience. In this case, it was not even to be contemplated. Whatever was between them must be nipped in the bud at once!

Cameron was the one to watch, Betsy thought shrewdly. He had a certain reckless impatience. From early childhood, as the eldest child and first son, he had never been refused anything his parents could provide him or his own beguiling nature might win him. He was also strong, adventurous, and passionate. With years he might become disciplined and cautious, like Duncan, his father . . . but not yet.

And Lorabeth, for all her gentle manner, must have a rebellious streak in her as well. Hadn't she flaunted her own mother's wishes and run away to Virginia by herself?

Betsy knew, without a doubt, that this dangerous

attraction must be diverted at once. So in a while, she beckoned Lorabeth from the harpsichord, ordered tea brought in, and launched an elaborate discussion of the gowns they must have Madame Luisa stitch for Lorabeth's trousseau. It was a subject designed to quickly dispel a man's ardor and send him to the limits of his patience.

Stifling a yawn, Cameron pleaded weariness and an early departure for Montclair the next morning and bade them all good night, knowing his own way to the guest bedroom.

To her concealed dismay, Betsy noticed that after Cameron left the room, Lorabeth wilted visibly, the shining look on her face fading as if someone had removed a mask.

Oh dear, thought Betsy, this impossible notion may have gone further than she had imagined. The best thing would be to set an early date for Lorabeth's marriage to Blakely. Too, she might drop a careful hint to Noramary that it might be well to urge that Cameron's wedding to Malinda not be delayed indefinitely.

Marriages, when they were carefully arranged, when the partners were well-suited to each other by birth, breeding, and family, were for the most part the best possible situation for both man and woman. Love, actually, had little to do with it, so Betsy believed. Common goals, determination to create a good home for the children they had, to provide a name with an honorable place in society—these were of utmost importance. Certainly not love. That fleeting emotion had caused more trouble in the world than anyone else knew.

Betsy sighed, folded up her embroidery, and announced she was ready to retire. Bleakly she wished she believed all those firm convictions, but too often she had seen a passionate love send all such firmly held convictions fleeing! Suddenly she felt her sixty-odd years.

Chapter 10

On the night of her birthday ball at Montclair, Lorabeth was met at the bottom of the curving stairway by her hosts, Noramary and Duncan Montrose, to join them in the receiving line.

"How lovely you look, my dear." Her aunt smiled, and turning to her tall husband, asked, "Doesn't she, Duncan?"

"A vision to behold!" declared the dignified master of Montclair.

Indeed Lorabeth did look lovely. Her gown, made especially for this occasion by the famed Williamsburg seamstress, Madame Luisa, was dusty rose taffeta, appliqued with a trail of silken apple-blossoms extending from one shoulder across the fitted bodice down the wide paniered skirt, draped to reveal a shirred pink underskirt.

Knowing from his wife that Uncle Duncan was a man of few words and rare compliments, Lorabeth felt warm with pleasure. To cover her sudden confusion, Lorabeth said quickly.

"And *you* look *beautiful,* Aunt Noramary."

"She *always* does!" agreed Uncle Duncan, with an affectionate glance at his tiny wife softening his rather stern expression.

His remark, surprisingly, caused her aunt to blush, and Lorabeth realized that even if theirs was an "arranged marriage" twenty years ago, these two were deeply in love.

Perhaps that was possible, Lorabeth mused thoughtfully as she took her place beside her aunt on the wide veranda in front of the open doors to the house. Perhaps love could follow even a marriage such as Noramary's and Duncan's. Aunt Laura had told her that at the time of Winnie's elopement, Noramary and a young Williamsburg neighbor had an "understanding." But when she had been asked to become the "substitute bride" by the distraught Barnwells, she had given him up to "do her duty." Looking at Noramary now, so secure and happy in Duncan's obvious adoration, she certainly did not seem to have any regrets. Maybe that was the best way. To do one's duty, do what you were called upon to do. After all, Scripture reminded: "All things work together for good to them that love God, to them who are called according to his purpose."

I must remember that, Lorabeth admonished herself, concealing her private misery behind a bright smile and gracious manner as the guests began to arrive.

But the heartache within was a heavy burden. Cameron had been nowhere to be seen since her arrival at Montclair that afternoon. Maybe he wouldn't show up at all!

Finally, unable to suppress her burning curiosity, she inquired of her aunt. "Where is Cameron? Isn't he coming to my party?"

"Of course, dear," Noramary assured her. "He wouldn't miss it. Early this morning he rode over to Woodlawn, the Drapers' plantation, and will be returning this evening to escort Malinda to the ball."

Lorabeth tried to stem her rush of disappointment. Cameron, coming with Malinda. But, of course! Naturally he would be escorting his fiancée.

A short time later an open carriage came to a

stop in front, and Lorabeth immediately recognized Mrs. Draper, fussily swathed in netting covering an elaborate powdered coiffure. Then she saw Cameron and her heart nearly stopped. He stepped down from the carriage to assist Mrs. Draper, then hand down Malinda, who looked like a yellow butterfly in yards of tulle.

Lorabeth watched Malinda make an imperious gesture and Cameron shook his head. Then, with a toss of her curls, she placed her hand on his arm and they mounted the steps together.

At Cameron's approach, Lorabeth felt a spreading warmth. Then she went cold all over. It was like the fever she had contracted the summer she was twelve. Her hands turned icy, her wrists weak, her legs unsteady. She struggled to maintain her composure as Cameron bowed, lifted her small, cold fingers to his lips, and wished her, "Happy Birthday, Lorabeth."

His eyes moved over her upturned face slowly, almost as if they were caressing her, lingering on her mouth like a kiss. He was so close she was newly aware of his eyes, the strong line of his jaw, the way his russet hair grew back from the high, broad forehead. His nearness made her quite breathless.

"You *will* save me a dance?" he asked her, smiling, although his eyes were serious.

"Of course," Lorabeth replied lightly, conscious of Malinda's annoyed frown puckering her smooth white brow.

"Maybe I best make sure. Let me have your dance card," Cameron suggested.

She handed him the small, tasseled card and, with a kind of reckless abandon, he scribbled his initials on three lines. When he returned it, their eyes met in a silent affirmation of what they were both feeling.

Pointedly, Malinda slipped her hand through Cameron's arm, then, smiling at Lorabeth with cloying sweetness, wished her a "Happy Birthday" and led Cameron away.

Feeling irrationally forsaken, Lorabeth's eyes followed them until she caught Aunt Laura gazing at her with anxious speculation. Lorabeth hoped desperately her aunt was not able to read her mind.

In a few minutes, distraction in the form of the arrival of Blakely and his parents, provided Lorabeth a welcome release.

"You look unbelievably beautiful!" Blakely told her adoringly as he bent over her hand. "I feel I am the most fortunate man in the world tonight."

Smiling fondly at them, Aunt Noramary whispered to Lorabeth that she was excused to go along with Blakely to begin the dancing. Happily Blakely drew her hand through his and clasping it warmly, led her into the large parlor that had been cleared of furniture, the floor waxed for dancing.

They moved gracefully into the promenade. Beaming at Lorabeth, Blakely said, "I'm so proud and happy, dearest. I cannot wait much longer to announce my happiness to the world. Mama and my father are delighted and will be speaking to your grandmother later this evening."

Lorabeth smiled at him vaguely. As he led her in the intricate steps of the minuet, her efforts to focus on him were dissipated by her realization that the couple dancing next to them was Malinda and Cameron.

Why, she asked herself, had God brought her and Cameron together at all, if only to keep them apart? Once more she felt an unhappy helplessness. Her abstraction must have been evident, for Blakely broke into her wandering thoughts reproachfully.

"You're not listening, Lorabeth."

"Sorry, Blakely. What was it?" She willed her attention back to him.

"Never mind, my darling. We'll have time to slip away and be together at supper. Besides, the dance is ending now, and here comes your next partner."

There were two others before Cameron, at last, appeared to claim Lorabeth for his dance. He extended his arm, his eyes grave, his mouth smiling. Facing each other on the dance floor, they spoke not a word, mutely following the steps precisely to the measure of the music. But they held each other in a rapt gaze. Immersed in each other, yet very conscious they were not alone, they moved within the pattern of the dance, touching each other only as it was choreographed. Because they dared not utter what was in their hearts, they were bonded in silence.

When the music stopped, Cameron bowed; Lorabeth curtsied. Still no word had passed between them. Only their reeling senses and pounding pulses gave tell-tale evidence of their inner feelings.

Even in the misty realm in which she floated, Lorabeth knew she should put all thoughts of him from her. It was Blakely she should be thinking about, not Cameron. Blakely—eminently eligible, hand-picked by her grandmother. Blakely who unquestionably adored her and was the ultimate means of her escape from her mother's plans. What useless fantasy to dream of Cameron. If it had not been for Blakely, it was very likely Lorabeth would already be packed aboard a ship to England—and Willie Fairchild!

The last dance before supper was Cameron's and, instead of leading her onto the dance floor again, he tucked her arm through his and guided her out through the French windows onto the shadowed porch.

As soon as they were outside, Cameron's hand tightened on her wrist and he hurried her to the far side of the veranda, down the steps and into the garden. The air was heavy with the scent of late-blooming roses. A safe distance from the lights of the house, with only the faint sound of the music drifting out to them, Cameron took Lorabeth in his arms. He held her for a long moment, so tightly she could feel his heart beating against her own.

"We must talk, Lorabeth. Alone. There's no time to waste. Listen, darling"—his voice was low and husky—"after everyone has gone, wait until the grandfather clock in the hall strikes two . . . then meet me here."

"But Cameron, we can't—"

He pressed his fingers lightly over her mouth to halt the flow of protest.

"Don't say 'no,' Lorabeth. It is of utmost importance . . ."

She started to say something else, but his mouth quieted hers in a kiss so sweetly tender that she lost all thought of denying him. The moment seemed to last for an eternity in which the world spun with a dizzying joy.

Then they heard a voice calling from the porch, and they broke apart as Aunt Laura came to the edge of the veranda.

Seeing them, she said, "Lorabeth, it's time for you to open your presents, dear."

"I'll give you mine later, when you meet me," Cameron whispered as they went up the steps together.

* * *

Lorabeth stood behind her half-open bedroom door, breathlessly awaiting the deep-toned striking of the clock. One. Two.

She took a long, shaky breath. Then, carrying her pink satin slippers, one in each hand, she moved like a shadow down the stairway, across the front hall.

There was a slight movement near the lilac bushes, and she halted, standing absolutely still, not daring to move or breathe. Then, out of the darkness, Cameron appeared.

Without speaking, he took her hand and led her to the side of the house, through the gate, and into his mother's English garden. In the pale light of the silvery new moon, the garden was magic. Once safe inside its walls, Cameron settled Lorabeth on the bench within the little latticed arched enclosure.

His own tension transferred itself to her. Her whole body trembled, her heart beat wildly, her hands were cold, and her breath shallow. She knew they were on the brink of danger in this secret meeting. But now she was powerless to avoid whatever might be its outcome.

Cameron drew a long breath, then spoke in a low, urgent voice. "I love you, Lorabeth. I know I've no right to speak to you of this. I'm not free. I know because we are related, that such an idea would shock the family. Wait! Hear me out." He held up his hand as if warning her not to interrupt. "Maybe it was meant to be. Maybe it was part of God's plan for both our lives. Why else would you have come halfway round the world? Why else would we have met if not for some reason—some divine purpose?"

Lorabeth shook her head, bewildered at his impetuousness.

"Don't deny it, Lorabeth. I think you feel the same way. Don't you love me, too?" Not waiting for her answer, he rushed on. "Whatever you say, I see it in your eyes."

"Oh, Cam, don't!" she begged. "It cannot be. It is too late. You're engaged to Malinda. And— tonight—well, it is practically settled. Grandmother agreed to Blakely's proposal and—" The tightness of her throat choked out the next words. "Besides . . . under the circumstances . . . it would never be allowed."

Cameron shook his head impatiently. "One thing at a time. All that can be worked out, I'm sure. It will just take time and *patience*, which is *not* one of my virtues." He paused with a half-smile as he added ruefully, "In fact, impatience, impulsiveness are my worst flaws. But this is too important to me. And I'll have to learn patience. Pray for it!" Again he halted. "I'm wildly impatient now to declare my love for you before the whole world!"

At this he put his arm around her waist and gently drew her to him. He tilted her slightly resisting chin upward, then slowly, with infinite tenderness kissed her. For a timeless moment the world rocked, then became quite still. Lorabeth looked up at Cam's face, illuminated by the newly risen moon, searching hers for an answer. Her resistance melted and she lifted her lips once more for his kiss.

"Don't you *know* now, Lorabeth?" he whispered softly as he cradled her gently. "I *do,* and *whatever* it takes—time, tact, *patience*—I will practice it, learn it, *pray* for it. It is worth whatever I have to do. Because it's you I love, and you I must have!"

In his arms she felt cherished, protected. Against her breast she could feel the heavy beat of his heart. She sighed, feeling the strength of his arms enfolding her.

If for this kiss alone, Lorabeth had traveled thousands of miles—if only for this one moment of happiness, she would gladly have traveled ten thousand more.

Slowly they drew apart and Cameron sighed. "Oh, my very dear, somehow we must sort this out. It simply has to be. I cannot imagine life without you now."

Lorabeth found her voice at last. "Cameron, you know it is impossible," she said sadly. "It was foolish for me to meet you here—"

He jumped to his feet, still clasping her hands.

"I can't accept that. I won't," he declared.

Startled by his vehemence, Lorabeth put a restraining hand on his.

"Cam, listen to me. We're both promised to others. We've given our word. Too many people would be hurt and disappointed. And there's more. So much more. You don't know that Grandmother Barnwell has staked her own honor on my betrothal to Blakely. You see, when I came to Virginia I was running away."

He made a gesture as if to protest, but she hurried on.

"Yes, it's true. If I had stayed in England, I would be married now. My mother had arranged a marriage I could not tolerate. So, when I told Grandmother—Blakely was already courting me—she wrote to my mother telling her my marriage to him would be a prestigious one, better even than the one *she* herself had planned. So you see, Grandmother and Blakely saved me, actually *ransomed* me, from a situation that was worse than you can imagine. There is no way I can go back now."

He stared at her, then shook his head in disbelief. "It doesn't matter," he said stubbornly. "I love you. I won't give you up so easily." He caught her to him so that her face was pressed against the rough lace of his jabot. "I can't lose you, Lorabeth— not *now!* I can't imagine living without you!"

"But you have—all these years."

"I didn't know what I was missing, that someone like you even existed. I thought what I was getting was all there is. That everyone's marriage is a kind of compromise—"

"Not your father and mother's," she reminded him gently.

"Yes, but they're different, special."

She tried to pull away but he only held her closer.

"It was a mistake for me to come out here," she said quietly, firmly. "We must go back in, Cam."

He held her for a moment longer, then with a sigh, released her. Fumbling in his waistcoat pocket, he drew out a small box and handed it to Lorabeth.

"Wait, at least, until I give you your birthday present."

She took it with trembling hands.

"What is it?" she asked tremulously, for it looked like a jewel case and she was afraid to see the contents.

"Open it."

She untied the ribbon and the silk cloth that wrapped it, removed the lid, and found inside a small porcelain box adorned with two delicately painted birds.

"A trinket box! How lovely!"

"No, it's a music box. It's best you don't lift the lid just now," he explained. "But every time you hear its melody, it will remind you that I love you, Lorabeth. Now and forever."

"Oh, Cameron, we are deceiving ourselves if we think . . ." As she held up her hand as if to wave away any more useless argument, the moonlight picked up the sparkle of the sapphire ring on her third finger, left hand. Almost as an afterthought, she held it out to show Cameron. "Blakely gave me this tonight in front of Grandmother, Aunt Laura, and his parents. And I accepted it, Cam. There's nothing either of us can do now."

"There must be. There *has* to be." Cameron's voice grew rough with emotion. "We'll find a way."

The moon moved across the sky from behind the sheltering trees, and the two of them were suddenly enveloped in moonlight. As if on cue, they put their arms out simultaneously and clung together, heart beating against heart, the bitter-sweetness of the moment too deep for any words. It was as if they knew they had to seize this moment before the reality of their situation crashed against them.

At last, reluctantly, they released each other.

"Believe me, my darling," Cameron repeated, "we'll find a way."

Lorabeth checked the reply she knew she should make. For now, she would just savor this precious time they had shared. Nothing would be changed by this clandestine meeting, this secret declaration of their love. Tomorrow, Cameron would still be engaged to Malinda; she, promised to Blakely. And, of course, they would always be cousins—bonded by the familial tie that sealed a lover's doom.

Chapter 11

Lorabeth let herself back into the house cautiously, tiptoed up the stairs along the upper hall and back into her room. She shut the door noiselessly, leaning against it for a moment as a shuddering sigh escaped her.

Slowly she turned around, then gave a horrified gasp when she saw a figure silhouetted by the moonlight. It was Aunt Laura, seated on the window seat in the recessed alcove.

At first Lorabeth could neither move nor speak.

"Aunt Laura! What are you doing here?"

"I couldn't sleep. I was overtired, overstimulated from the party. My room seemed too warm. I got up to open the window. Then I saw you—and Cameron—in the garden." Her voice faltered. Then she rose and came toward Lorabeth, holding out her arms. "Oh, my poor dear."

Something inside Lorabeth crumbled. For the first time since her arrival in Virginia, she felt she could drop the facade she had so carefully erected. She went into her aunt's arms and let herself be comforted.

When her sobs diminished, she dried her tears, and with some effort poured out the story of her love for Cameron, of his for her.

"It took us both completely by surprise. It was so unexpected. We felt it almost from the first, but it wasn't until tonight—"

"But tonight you accepted Blakely's ring." Aunt Laura shook her head in distress.

"I know! I know!" Lorabeth exclaimed desperately, putting up both hands to cover burning cheeks. "It was wrong. It was all wrong! But tonight, when Malinda was flaunting Cameron so, I was filled with envy—"

"Envy is a sin!" Aunt Laura said in a shocked whisper.

"Yes, I know that too, and I confess it. I envy

everything about her. I envy her beauty, her manner, her lovely clothes, her wealth. Mostly I envy her— Cameron!" Lorabeth put her face in her hands.

"But he's your cousin, dear. Any romantic thoughts of Cameron—well, it's impossible, you know," Laura said with finality.

"Oh, Aunt Laura—tonight it *did* seem possible! Maybe it was the excitement of the evening, the music, the gaiety. The fact that it was my birthday. Somehow it all seemed within my reach—"

"But, my dear, think of the consequences. All the lives involved in such folly. Certainly you knew better than to think anything could come of such an attachment?"

"Yes, I knew better, Aunt Laura. I've known all along. And I've tried—really I have. But knowledge and trying doesn't keep one from dreaming. . . ."

Laura put out her hand in a comforting gesture.

But Lorabeth shook her head and, straightening her slim shoulders, drew a long shaky breath.

"I knew better, but I'm afraid I couldn't help loving Cameron. Now I suppose I must pay the price." She turned her tear-stained face to Aunt Laura's kind searching look. "I hope—*pray*—it will never happen again. I wouldn't want to hurt anyone."

"Then we must leave first thing in the morning," Aunt Laura said decisively—"before Cameron does anything rash. And you must promise, my dear, that you will not allow such a meeting to take place again. For both your sakes. You *do* promise, don't you, Lorabeth?"

Lorabeth nodded. "You're right, of course, Aunt Laura, and I promise. But it will be so hard."

"You are strong, Lorabeth. Look at what you've done already, how much you've survived! For many reasons you must be stronger still. Perhaps even stronger than Cameron. He does not know what it is like to be denied anything. He is a fine young man with many good qualities . . . but he lacks discipline. What he wants, he *will* have. You must be the one, Lorabeth, to be wise, to do the *right* thing, the *best* thing for everyone concerned."

Tears crowded Lorabeth's eyes, rolling down her cheeks unchecked. "Weren't you ever in love, Aunt Laura?"

There was a short silence, then her aunt patted Lorabeth's hand sympathetically. "Oh, yes, my dear. I was. Never think that I cannot understand."

"Why, then, did you never marry?" Lorabeth asked the question she had longed to ask.

"There was a terrible misunderstanding, never resolved. And he married someone else." She paused. "After him—well, I never found anyone else I could love."

"Maybe, for some women, it is like that," Lorabeth said solemnly. "Maybe there is only one love in a lifetime."

"But that doesn't mean you cannot have a successful marriage, Lorabeth," Aunt Laura reminded her gently. "For me, it wasn't necessary to marry. My father left me my own inheritance. But for someone like you, my dear . . ." Her voice trailed off. What she had been about to say was painfully obvious.

Promising to make all the necessary explanations and arrangements to return to Williamsburg early the next day, Aunt Laura went back to her own bedroom. Lorabeth sat for a long time at the window gazing out into the darkness, knowing that the memory of this night would haunt her forever.

Aunt Laura had spoken gently, but the harsh reality remained that Lorabeth really had no alternative. She was a woman alone in the world, with no security, no family. She was utterly defenseless. Blakely would be a good, faithful, devoted husband. The Ashfords were kind and had welcomed their son's choice graciously, even though she was coming to him without dowry or property.

But Lorabeth knew the bitter truth. She did not love Blakely as she should, for her heart was already given to another man and would be his forever, no matter what the outer circumstances of her life.

Lorabeth buried her face in her hands and the tears poured down her cheeks, trickling through her fingers onto the beautiful dress. Finally, she slipped to her knees, knowing only God could help her bear what must be borne.

For what purpose had He brought her safely to America, to Virginia? Perhaps, after all, it was to make this good, solid marriage to Blakely. It could not have been to break every tradition of society and the church, to fall in love with a cousin, already engaged, whom she would never be allowed to marry even if he were free.

"Oh, dear Lord, whatever is Your will for my life, I accept it. I promise—from this day forward—to put away all foolish, vain longings for something—*someone* who does not belong to me and never can. Help me to be conformed to Your will."

Even as the pinkish-gray light of dawn crept through the window, a strange kind of peace pervaded Lorabeth's spirit. Although her heart still felt like a bruised, battered weight within her, she knew what she must do. All the lovely possibilities of the night before in the garden with Cameron vanished with the moonlight.

Aunt Laura was right. She and Cameron should never have declared themselves. She must return to Williamsburg before any further damage was done.

But she could not leave without some word to him—"a word well-chosen" to close the dangerous door they had opened, to release him from any rashly made promise.

Lorabeth got out of bed, found some paper in the escritoire by the window overlooking the garden where only the night before they had held each other. Biting her lip, she thought for a moment, then dipped the quill into the inkwell and began to write.

When she had finished, she folded the paper and, opening the bedroom door to see that the hallway was empty, tiptoed along the passage to Cameron's room. There she dropped the note on the floor and carefully slipped it under his door.

When Lorabeth, Grandmother, and Aunt Laura were ready to leave Montclair the next morning, Cameron was nowhere in sight. It was accepted by his family that the young man came and went as he chose, so no one took special note of his absence. In her troubled heart, however, Lorabeth felt he did not dare tell her goodbye in front of the others. For that she was thankful. She could not have trusted herself, either, not to betray their forbidden bond.

Aunt Noramary had accepted Aunt Laura's excuse that they must get back to Williamsburg immediately to begin making the preparations for Lorabeth's trousseau and wedding.

"The Ashfords are anxious to set a date and, no wonder, when they will be getting such a lovely daughter-in-law." She smiled at Lorabeth indulgently. "And," she added mischievously, "I've never seen a bridegroom-to-be more ready to leave off bachelorhood than Blakely!"

Lorabeth could not help wondering what her aunt would think if she knew what had taken place in her very garden, and felt fresh shame.

Back in Williamsburg plans for the wedding proceeded with frightening rapidity. Grandmother Barnwell and Aunt Laura were busy from morning till night, making lists of all kinds. The trousseau was of paramount importance. Ashford was a proud and prominent Virginia name, and any young woman marrying into their family would be expected to have an extensive and elaborate wardrobe.

There were endless sessions with Madame Luisa. Or so it seemed to Lorabeth. The noted seamstress, ever mindful of her reputation, was a perfectionist, and every detail of her creations had to be flawless, down to the last inch of trimming. She would sketch, then discard, then present a new design, explaining in detail each fold of drapery, each cut of a sleeve or bodice. The two Barnwell ladies were fascinated and wholly absorbed. But Lorabeth, used to twice-turned skirts and made-over dresses for most of her life, found the proceedings tedious.

She did not often allow herself the luxury of thinking about Cameron. But there were moments of despair when the need to see him again was insistent. What was he doing now? What was he feeling or thinking? Sometimes she felt as if their brief encounters, so intensely rich and meaningful, would serve her for a lifetime. At other times, confronted by the thought of long years without him, her courage failed her and she wept for what could never be. Over and over, she resolved steadfastly to put aside all further thought of him.

At those times she sought the comfort of the strengthening words of Psalms. In David's prayers for protection against his enemies, Lorabeth found enormous identification. Her love for Cameron was her enemy; the constant temptation to throw off restraint, to give in and abandon herself to their forbidden alliance.

On her knees the battle was daily waged and won.

Although Grandmother Barnwell noted Lorabeth's wan expression, her lassitude and loss of appetite, she put it down to pre-wedding doldrums. All young girls suffered such symptoms, Betsy assured herself, and only reminded Lorabeth of the fine match she was making.

To complicate matters, letters from Winnie, filled with recriminations, reproach, and stinging accusations, arrived almost weekly. Lorabeth was accustomed to such scoldings in person, but seeing them written in her mother's slashing handwriting made them seem even more shattering. In her letters Winnie repeated the cruel remarks she had often told Lorabeth verbally, that she was an "ungrateful, deceitful, and disobedient girl."

Grandmother barely skimmed the letters. "Humph! What mother could want more than for her daughter to marry into one of Virginia's first families? Blakely is not only one of the finest young gentlemen in the county, but one of the wealthiest. He will inherit both from his mother and father. His mother was a Sedgewick on her mother's side and a Llewellyn on her father's, and brought both wealth and property when she married Squire Ashford. You will be very well set, my dear, and why should Winnie not rejoice at that?"

Lorabeth had no answer.

"Winnie is simply having a tantrum on paper! Once she meets Blakely and his family and sees their manner of living, she'll change her tune. Then all will be forgiven and soon forgotten as far as you're concerned. So don't fret, my dear. I've told Winnie she is to come to Virginia at my expense to attend her daughter's wedding, and we shall all have a pleasant, happy reunion."

Lorabeth was not so sure, knowing how her mother harbored grudges and nurtured unforgiveness. But until it was known if Winnie was coming, no wedding date would be set.

Blakely was in constant attendance. Although this in itself was a distraction for Lorabeth, it was also an increasing source of anxiety. Was it fair to him to give him only half her heart, mind, and soul? Knowing he might possess her body but never know her spirit plunged Lorabeth into periods of great distress.

Blakely, however, seemed content. Not knowing what she regretfully withheld from him, he happily escorted Lorabeth everywhere, eager to show off the "English beauty" he had won.

When she was not with Blakely, Lorabeth was most often at one of the interminable fittings. Returning from Madame Luisa's one afternoon, she found the house quiet. Betsy was napping, she discovered upon peeping into her bedroom, and Aunt Laura must be making social calls.

Fighting melancholy, Lorabeth decided to go into the music room. The harpsichord had always proven an antidote for dejected spirits. Pausing in front of the hall mirror to remove her bonnet, she became aware of another reflection. Startled, she whirled about to find Cameron standing in the doorway.

"I had to see you," he said in a low, tense voice.

"But, you shouldn't have . . ."

She stood staring at him, unable to speak or

move. On one level of consciousness she longed to fly into his arms; on the other, she wished for escape. She was like a moth inexorably drawn to a flame, sensing its danger, yet willing to risk that danger.

"We *must* talk, Lorabeth."

"It's no use, Cameron."

Lorabeth had not seen him since the night of her birthday ball. The only reminder of that enchanted evening was the small music box he had given her. She had hidden it in one of the drawers of the applewood chest in her bedroom, only daring to take it out when she was by herself, lest someone hear its sweet, tinkling melody.

There was a pounding in her temples and her heart was beating uncomfortably fast. Still, she hesitated.

It was Cameron who, at last, made the decision. With a few purposeful strides he walked over to the door of the music room, thrust it open, and motioned her forward.

Meekly Lorabeth followed him into the room. Quickly she moved behind the love seat, placing both hands on its back, bracing herself behind this safe barricade.

"You should not have come and I should not be receiving you alone. This is folly, Cameron."

"I've come, Lorabeth, because I've thought and thought about this and I finally had to act. You must not rush into this marriage with Blakely before we can work things out. My mother told me you are waiting to hear if Aunt Winnie is coming before setting a date. In the meantime, I will explain to Malinda and—"

"Oh, no, Cameron, you mustn't!" Lorabeth cried out, thoroughly alarmed.

"But I *must*. I don't love Malinda. I love *you*! I can't marry someone I don't love, and neither can *you*! Where is the honor in that?"

"There is no use discussing this as though there could be a future for us. You are forgetting the most important point of all—we are *first cousins*! We cannot marry. Our families would be horrified! The church would never condone—"

"Blast it all, Lorabeth! We can elope, find someone who would marry us. The Church of England isn't the only church authorized to perform a marriage ceremony!"

"You can't mean what you're saying! What about your family. . . . You're the oldest son, the heir to Montclair. You can't abandon your responsibilities, your inheritance, your duty!"

"I have two younger brothers. In a few years, either of them could learn to run the plantation—eventually take over . . ."

But into the confident tone he had used earlier had crept a note of uncertainty. Lorabeth heard it immediately and knew she had struck a sensitive area.

"Cameron, I said everything I felt in the note I

wrote to you before leaving Montclair. You must accept it. There is no way for us. The best, the bravest, the kindest thing we can do for each other is to help each other bear it."

Lorabeth struggled to hold back the tears that rushed into her eyes, and clenched her hands until the nails dug into the soft flesh of her palms. She managed a wistful smile as Cameron fixed his gaze upon her.

Knowing she was near the breaking point, Lorabeth knew she must get out of his sight, away from the refuge his arms might hold for her if she yielded.

She moved from behind the love seat and started toward the door. But to reach it, she had to pass him. He effectively prevented this maneuver by stepping squarely into her path. He then stretched one arm across the door and, leaning toward her, placed the other hand on her waist. He was so near she could see his eyes, the dark pupils, the stubby lashes.

He drew in his breath sharply and, with something like a moan, gathered her to him. "Oh, my darling, how can I let you go?"

In spite of herself Lorabeth clung to him.

"I can't, I *won't* let this happen to us!" Cameron's voice was ragged. "How can we live without each other?"

Sobs tore at her throat as finally, with all the strength at her command, Lorabeth pulled herself out of his embrace. "Only with God's help, Cameron!"

With that, she turned and fled through the door, across the hall and up the steps, never once looking back at the stricken young man.

Chapter 12

The first part of October, called "Indian Summer" by Virginians, boasted warm, sunny days and crisp evenings. Morning fires were needed in the fireplaces of all the rooms in the Barnwell house to dispel the lingering chill.

On one such morning, Lorabeth sat propped up in bed watching Odelia, Essie's niece, stir the ashes of last night's fire before starting a new one. Being waited on was still an unaccustomed luxury, one that Lorabeth found difficult to accept.

So she rested uneasily against the plump pillows, sipping the cup of chocolate Odelia had brought her, and tried to exercise patience. She would have to heed Odelia's warning, "to wait 'til it's good and warm 'fore you venture out of baid. Dey is frost on de groun' dis mawnin'." At least she would wait until the young maid left, Lorabeth decided.

There was an extra reason for Lorabeth's restlessness this particular morning. The day before something had happened that weighed heavily on her heart.

In the afternoon Blakely's mother had come to call on Grandmother Barnwell. The intent of her visit was soon apparent. With well-mannered curiosity she had inquired as to whether Lorabeth's mother would be attending the wedding. She did so want to give the young couple a prenuptial party. But, until she knew when the date was to be, well—Mrs. Ashford had sighed and flung out her dainty hands in a hopeless gesture.

There had been an ominous silence from England since the invitation to her daughter's wedding was dispatched to Winnie. All Grandmother could do was to cover her own irritation at Winnie's failure to reply with her usual optimism. She spoke of a Christmas wedding or, "If not then, spring is always a beautiful time for a wedding, don't you agree?"

Mrs. Ashford had left in a rather unsettled frame of mind, and Lorabeth herself felt vaguely unhappy. Only Betsy maintained her determinedly cheerful attitude. Things had proceeded according to her plans thus far, and she had no reason to believe, despite Winnie's petulance, that everything would not work out well.

After Mrs. Ashford left, Lorabeth had climbed the stairs to her room. She did not wish to have to explain her strange mood, caused by the underlying reason for her unhappiness.

When alone, she had taken from its hiding place the music box Cam had given her. Cradling it in her hands, she lifted its lid to listen to the melody. She seated herself on the window seat and, while the merry little tune played, she looked out at the bare trees against a blue-gray sky and watched a flock of birds in a rushing V streak across it. The music box ran down, and with a sigh, Lorabeth closed the top, a forlorn emptiness filling her heart.

Just then the door opened and Odelia peeked in, looking about. Seeing that Lorabeth was alone, she advanced into the room and handed her an envelope, whispering conspiratorially, "Mr. Cam lef' it fo' you, Miss Lorabeth. Say doan tell nobody. Jes' be sure yo' got it when yo' was by yo'sef. Say I was to gib yo' answer to young Micah, and he would carry it to Mr. Cam at de Raleigh Tavern. He waitin' dere 'til yo' send him word."

Lorabeth took the envelope with hands that shook and read it hastily.

> Lorabeth, I have to see you. It is of utmost importance. Where can I meet you so we may talk privately? I beg you not to refuse.—C.

She knew the right thing, the sensible thing, would be to send Micah, his messenger boy, back to the Raleigh with the word IMPOSSIBLE scribbled across the bottom of his note. Still, Lorabeth hesitated.

What now could be "of utmost importance"? Hadn't they said all that could be said, only to part at an impasse? The only honorable solution was renunciation. What could possibly come of their seeing each other again—what, but more pain? Nothing had or could change their circumstances. Not even God Himself could alter the conditions of their birth.

But the thought of being with Cam for even a short time was so overwhelming that, in the next moment, she was scribbling a note under Cam's signature: "I have an appointment at 10 tomorrow morning at Madame Luisa's."

It was done. Guiltily she refolded the note, placed it in its envelope, and handed it back to Odelia. She was sure Cam would find a way to meet her there.

Now, in the light of this clear October morning,

Lorabeth regretted her rash decision. She should have resisted her longing to see Cam. Nothing but further heartache could result. But it would be pointless to try to get another message to Cameron now.

As she dressed, Lorabeth was nearly sick with guilt. She hated dishonesty in any form, yet it seemed much of her life lately had been marked by deception. She dreaded to think what her grandmother, and especially Aunt Laura, would make of what she was doing this day.

Heavy-hearted, Lorabeth started out for her appointment at Madame Luisa's, accompanied by Odelia. She had one moment of stark terror when Aunt Laura considered coming along. Then an unexpected caller arrived, and she had to stay at home.

Though the shop was only a short walk from the Barnwell house, to Lorabeth it felt as if it were a thousand miles. With each step her conscience reproached her, even while her defiant heart rejoiced at the thought of even this stolen time with Cam.

Lorabeth could not imagine on what pretext Cameron had convinced Madame Luisa's servant to let him wait in the small sitting room where she found him when she was ushered in. She was aware of little else but her own heart's frantic beat and the joy she felt at seeing his tall figure standing by the fireplace.

In a few long strides he was at her side, took both her hands in his, and pressed them to his chest.

"I was afraid you might not come," he said, his eyes sweeping over her as if memorizing every detail of her appearance. "How lovely you are. I've starved for the sight of you."

She drew her hands from his firm clasp. "I shouldn't have. . . ." She shook her head in dismay at her own foolhardiness.

Cameron ignored her protest. "Listen, my darling," he began, rushing on. "There's still time. We have two choices open to us. The truth is the most direct way. Simply go to your grandmother, my parents, tell them we are in love and that we want to be married. Of course, they will offer all sorts of objections. Malinda's pride will be hurt, but little else. Her feelings for me are of the most shallow sort, and can be just as easily bestowed on some other willing man. Auntie B. may be upset after all her maneuverings to "ransom' you from your mother's arrangements, but only temporarily. I think she would be on our side. Blakely, poor lad—but all's fair in love and war. No matter, it is far better for two engagements to be broken than for four people to marry the wrong partners and live in misery for the rest of their days!"

Lorabeth was speechless before his logic.

When she did not reply, Cameron went on,

"Of course, the other choice is much simpler. We just run off together—and right now!"

She stared at him numbly, twisting her hands in anguish. She was stunned by his recklessness, his daring, his lack of regard for consequences. It had been Cameron's sense of honor that had always been the bulwark against her own weakness. And even as everything inside her melted at the look of adoration in his eyes, the confidence in his voice, she began to shake her head. His dear face blurred through the tears that filled her eyes.

Lorabeth had always heard that a person sees his whole life pass before him in a moment of crisis. She saw now her mother's face in the dreadful scenes that followed Lorabeth's rejection of each suitor; next came Grandmother Barnwell's look of disappointment upon learning the truth; then, Aunt Laura's kind but reproachful one, followed by Blakely's cheerful countenance, his trusting eyes. One by one, all the people who would be shocked, hurt, disillusioned, crushed by the rash act Cameron was suggesting, flashed into her mind. The momentary exhilaration she had felt while caught up in Cam's excitement, the thought of escaping from all the pressures that weighed upon her, were swept away.

She put out one hand to touch Cam's arm and slowly shook her head. "We can't. You *know* we can't."

There was a taut pause. Cameron straightened his shoulders and snapped out his next words crisply. "All right then. It's hopeless to try to convince you."

He turned, picked up his tricorne from the table, and held it in front of him. His fingers kneading the brim were the only evidence of agitation as he spoke.

"You know what you're doing, Lorabeth, don't you? You're condemning us to a life sentence of regret. I hope you won't have cause to wish you'd decided otherwise.

"All I've ever wanted since I first met you and realized I loved you, was to protect you, care for you, see that you had everything to guarantee your happiness. In spite of everything, Lorabeth, I want you to be happy!"

At last, they looked at each other gravely—a long look filled with despair. It was as if they both knew that this moment would have to see them through a lifetime apart.

Then Cameron turned and walked out the door.

Chapter 13

It took every ounce of will power Lorabeth could summon to endure the seemingly endless fitting. While Madame Luisa and her assistants fluttered about her, fussing, plucking, nipping, pinning, and unpinning the length of satin and lace that was being molded to her lithe figure, Lorabeth's fists balled tightly. When she thought she could not bear another minute, Madame Luisa stood back, her head to one side, and made the final adjustment, to the awed approval of her sewing ladies.

"*Voila! C'est magnifique!*" they choroused.

Only then was Lorabeth released to leave.

Followed by Odelia, Lorabeth hurried along the road home, her head bent against a chill wind on a day turned suddenly dreary and gray.

The minute she stepped inside the front door, Lorabeth sensed an air of foreboding. The house, normally echoing the sounds of conversation and activity at this hour of the day, was unnaturally quiet.

She stood uncertainly in the hallway, listening. Taking a few steps, she paused at the door to the parlor and saw that her grandmother and Aunt Laura were seated there.

As she looked in, her grandmother beckoned to her.

"Come, Lorabeth. We've been waiting for you."

Lorabeth moved into the arch of the doorway, glancing anxiously from one to the other. Something in their expressions sent a ripple of apprehension along her spine. Slowly she entered the room.

Her Grandmother gathered an envelope and several sheets of paper from her lap and held them out to her. Lorabeth took the pages and saw the closely written lines, penned in her mother's familiar writing.

"This letter came from your mother by this morning's post. I think you should read it."

Lorabeth, her knees suddenly shaky, sat down on the edge of the sofa and began to read:

"My dear Mama, I take pen in hand with many misgivings and yet with the fervent hope that this letter will not reach you too late. As you can imagine, with Lorabeth's hasty departure, I have suffered the same distress you must have when, as a young and foolish girl, I ran off from my good home, leaving much havoc and heartache in my wake. Only a mother's heart could understand such suffering and I have certainly been punished for my own foolhardy behavior all these years. But we learn by our mistakes and so that is why I now hasten to reply to your letter just received concerning the impending marriage between Lorabeth and Blakely Ashford.

"Heaven knows I have tried to bring Lorabeth up with a sense of duty that she sadly seems to have abandoned, preferring to display only ingratitude for all I have done for her. A marriage such as I planned for her would have saved her from the disgrace that the information I am about to give you will cause her."

At this point Lorabeth looked up from the letter in bewilderment, glancing from her grandmother to Aunt Laura for some clue. Meeting only their impassive looks, she turned back to the letter, reading on.

"In *your* letter, dear mother, you implored me to forgive and forget Lorabeth's undisciplined and deceitful behavior in leaving England without my knowledge or permission. This I shall try to do. But to let you continue under the assumption that this engagement, which you are so happy about, is, and here I quote your very words, 'the celebration of a mutually appropriate, harmonious, prideful union of two of Virginia's finest families,' would be grossly unfair. Indeed, it would be a lie of the basest kind.

"To clarify what I am about to tell you, I must reveal shameful facts that I have long kept from you to protect your precious sensitivities, and to avoid hurting you and my dear, late father, even more than when I eloped with Phillippe Jouquet twenty years ago.

"To my sorrow, I learned too late what you tried to teach me as we were all growing up under your strict, but loving care—that 'we reap what we sow.' This I have done in full measure as my following confession will bear out.

"We had barely landed on English soil when I discovered it would be impossible for Phillippe to fulfill his promise—which was to marry me immediately in the first Anglican church we could find. Impossible because, he then told me to my horrified disbelief and shock, he already had a wife in France. Nothing could ever adequately describe to you, dear mother, my complete collapse at this information. Young, alone, my virtue gone, unable to return to my homeland or to my family who, for all I knew, had totally disowned me, what was I to do?

"Phillipe convinced me his wife would never consent to a divorce because of her religion. He swore to me that he had never loved her, that he had been coerced into the marriage, that the woman, several years his senior, had tricked him. He had come to America, he told me, to escape an insufferable situation. He swore he loved me, that even our unsanctified union was his only "real marriage.' All this may sound as though I am trying to justify my original error. I am only saying that it remained wrong and, as it turned out, ended in further sorrow and disgrace.

"However, try to imagine my plight—barely eighteen, alone except for this man, without family or friends, adrift in a strange country, afraid to write my parents the truth. Finally I was forced to accept my lot. Phillipe secured a position as French teacher at a boarding school about twenty miles south of London. With the position came a small cottage, and there we lived as man and wife. How was I to guess that, a little over a year later, he would do to me the same thing he had done to the unfortunate woman in France. Yes, dear mother, Phillipe 'eloped' again—this time with the wealthiest young lady at the school.

"I suppose Phillipe assumed I was a wealthy young American heiress when he persuaded me to run away with him. I believe he felt that eventually I would be 'reconciled' with my family and at least receive a 'comfortable allowance.' I could never prevail upon myself to tell you the true state of my situation, so of course, no 'allowance' was forthcoming. Phillipe, to whom the luxuries of life meant so much, soon tired of living on a school teacher's income, and when he saw the chance to use his charm on another unsuspecting victim, he did so with no remorse.

"Again, my dear mother, can you imagine my distress. Still young, although now thoroughly disillusioned, I was once more left alone, penniless, and disgraced. It was only through the kindness of the headmaster and his wife that I was not thrown upon the mercy of a heartless fate. They took me into their home as companion-helper to the wife, who was in a delicate condition. Sad to relate, this dear lady died in childbirth, leaving a motherless infant and a bereaved husband, himself without kith or kin.

"In this time of grief, I stayed to take care of the baby, remaining as a kind of housekeeper. For the sake of appearances, after the year of mourning, we married. He had been offered a new position as headmaster at another school, and I accompanied him there as his wife with 'our' baby daughter. As you may now have guessed, that baby was Lorabeth. When she was christened, poor Edgar was too stricken with the loss of his beloved wife, so I took care of all the arrangements, and it was I who chose her name—Laura Elizabeth.

"If you remember, I wrote you at the time of my marriage to Edgar Whitaker, telling you of Phillipe's 'death,' then waited an appropriate length of time before telling you of 'our' baby's birth. So actually Lorabeth is nearly a year older than you think.

"I know this will all come as a painful surprise, but I could not allow the real child of a humble English schoolmaster whose lineage is undistinguished, himself the son of a village vicar, to be passed off as a member of *our* family and be married to one of an equally prestigious Virginia family.

"I am sure you will appreciate learning the truth even after so long a time, and before you are yourself implicated in the fraudulent position of presenting Lorabeth to the Ashfords as your true granddaughter.

"Under these circumstances, you will, I am sure, send Lorabeth back to England at once to avoid any scandal following the quiet cancellation of her wedding plans there. I shall try, as I have done in the past, to do my best for her. To my great wonderment, especially after all the grief she has caused, Willie Fairchild is still willing to marry her.

"I want to get this letter to you by the next ship sailing to Virginia, so I shall now close. I remain as ever,

"Yr. affectionate daughter,

"Winnifred."

The pages of the letter fluttered to the floor from Lorabeth's numbed fingers.

"Poor Mama."

Lorabeth's unexpected words caused Betsy to give her a startled glance. This was not the reaction she might have expected after such staggering news.

"Now I understand so much," Lorabeth continued, so softly she might have been talking to herself. "No wonder she was frantic for me to make a good marriage. She knew what it was like to be alone with no one to depend on, without family or fortune." All at once Lorabeth identified with the frightened girl left abandoned in a strange country, the girl who had grown up to be her sharp-tongued, complaining mother—*step*-mother, she quickly corrected herself mentally. Even that made it more understandable. Saddled with a stubborn, willful child who was not even her own. How difficult her life must have been, Lorabeth sympathized.

"I suppose that rascal Jouquet thought our eldest daughter would have a handsome dowry. And when he discovered that dowry would naturally fall to Noramary, who took Winnie's place as Duncan

Montrose's bride, it must have come as quite a blow. Two wives and not a penny between them!" Grandmother said with some irony and a hint of satisfaction. Then matter-of-factly, she continued, "The task now is to break the news to the Ashfords that their son is not actually uniting with the Barnwell family. Not that it will make a mite of difference to Blakely nor to them either, if I'm right. Nonetheless, they must be told."

Lorabeth turned her wide eyes on Betsy, with an unspoken question she was not yet ready to frame.

But will it make a difference to you? Now that you know I'm not really your granddaughter? she pondered. *I don't belong here under your roof. I don't deserve all the kindnesses, the gracious provisions, the clothes, the affection, the full-hearted acceptance I have received from you! And now, the embarrassment of going to the family-conscious Ashfords, dragging out the almost-forgotten scandal of Winnie and its after-math, now blighting the pristine plans for a wedding of social importance!* At the thought, tears welled up, stinging her eyes.

"I think I'll go upstairs to my room for a while, Grandmother," Lorabeth said, getting to her feet. Then at the use of the now familiar name, she stopped in confusion. She lifted her hands in a pitiful gesture. "I mean—what shall I call you now?"

"Oh, for pity's sake, my dear! *Grandmother,*

what else? Wouldn't it be silly to start treating each other any differently now?" Betsy demanded.

Wordlessly Lorabeth turned and left the parlor.

Chapter 14

Lorabeth had not expected to sleep at all that night. Exhausted from weeping, however, she drifted off, awakening some time in the night to find the room bright with moonlight.

Slowly she raised herself from the crumpled pillows and from the bed where she had flung herself, fully clothed. She loosened her stays and undressed.

Donning a soft, woolen wrapper, she went to

the window seat and looked out. The garden was beautiful, bathed in a luminous glow. Then, before her eyes, the moon suddenly disappeared behind a cloud, blackening the sky. Lorabeth shivered and turned away.

The fuzziness of her deep yet troubled slumber gradually cleared, and she was again confronted with the problem she could no longer avoid. Earlier, she had escaped to her room to sob out her heart after reading the terrible letter. But there was no escape from the truth.

She was not just a "poor relation," but a penniless stranger, with no real home—not even in England! The person she had believed all these years to be her mother was only a woman who, in the interest of expediency, had taken on her care. For the first time Lorabeth understood Winnie's lack of warmth, her indifference toward her. What a burden she must have been to that sadly harassed lady!

Now, of course, she must decide what to do. She could not go on as if everything were the same, as if this startling information about her birth and her real ancestry were not known.

She certainly could not stay on here, imposing on the Barnwells' hospitality, expecting them to continue treating her as a member of the family.

Whatever was to be done must be done with the least amount of fuss, the least trouble for everyone. She felt a cold knot of misery twist inside her when she thought of Grandmother Barnwell and all the planning, the parties, the clothes that had been prepared in the belief that Lorabeth was her granddaughter. Perhaps the best way would be to slip away without painful partings, without any reproaches or false promises. Yes, that was the only thing left for her to do—to get out of the Barnwells' life as quickly as possible. There would be enough explaining to do even if she were not still here to be an embarrassment to them.

Somehow she must get back to England, Lorabeth decided. There she was sure to find a position as a governess or a teacher. She had mastered all the skills and accomplishments of a real lady and the experience of teaching when she was at Briarwood. She could then begin a new life where no one knew her or of her ill-fated sojourn in Virginia. She was certainly not going to impose further on Winnie—nor would she marry Willie Fairchild! From now on, she would make it on her own—as lonely and frightening a prospect as that might be.

But how was she to obtain money for her passage on a ship? And how was she to leave without anyone knowing? All these details must be worked out, and quickly, before anyone suspected. Speed was of utmost importance, for Lorabeth knew that Grandmother and Aunt Laura would never allow her to feel the impossibility of her position, nor make her feel uncomfortable in any way. In her fondness for them, she must spare them further distress.

Lorabeth paced restlessly—across the room, over to the bed, back to the window, then to the armoire, wringing her hands. As she did so, she absent-mindedly twisted her engagement ring. Suddenly she became aware of it. She took it off, examining it closely. Blakely had had the ring specially designed. It was a lovely sapphire, mounted with two small pansies fashioned of diamonds and emerald chips. It must be returned, of course, and Blakely released from their engagement immediately.

The ring! It must be very valuable. It was a large, flawless stone—a deep, rich, fiery blue— with small diamonds in the flowers. It must be worth a great deal of money, Lorabeth speculated.

She could pawn it to get money for her passage! The thought suddenly spun into her mind. She would do that at once. Then write Blakely a letter, enclosing the receipt so he could redeem the ring. By that time, if luck were with her, she would be on board a ship sailing out of Yorktown harbor and on the high seas. If she timed it just right, everything would work out satisfactorily for everyone.

Of course, Blakely would be hurt at first. But when she explained, she felt sure he would eventually understand that it was the only way. And he would find a more socially acceptable young lady to marry before too long. Yes, it was as if she had been given a way.

Her mind raced ahead. She would take nothing with her but the clothes she had brought here. She would pack her one small trunk and leave instructions that it be sent when she had a new address. At this point the bleakness of her situation momentarily overwhelmed her, and tears of self-pity flooded her eyes.

The thought of setting out alone again into the unknown was frightening. Here she had been loved, cherished, protected, had known the comfort of a loving family for the first time in her short life. It would be hard to forsake that sweet affection and once more be buffeted by the harsh coldness of the world.

Into her mind came the Scripture that had stood her in good stead nearly a year ago when she had first crossed the ocean to come to Virginia. It would sustain her now as she left. "I will never fail thee nor forsake thee." She had to trust God to guide her in the way she should go.

Sternly, Lorabeth dried her tears, told herself she must be brave. There was too much to do, too many things to take care of; she could not fall apart now.

In order to avoid detection, she would have to take someone into her confidence. But who? The only one she could think of was Odelia. But could the young maid keep a secret? And would she be willing to help?

She would have to take that chance, Lorabeth decided. Odelia was bright, clever, quick-witted, and she had become very fond of Lorabeth. But was her loyalty to the Barnwells stronger than any temporary promise Lorabeth might be able to elicit from her? She would have to see—to think of some way to pledge Odelia to secrecy, at least until she was safely away.

As it turned out, it was easier than Lorabeth had imagined it would be. The next morning when Odelia brought her her tray of chocolate and fresh rolls, Lorabeth fixed her with a solemn look.

"Odelia, you must give me your promise that you will do exactly what I say and tell no one anything. If you do so, I will give you a fine reward."

The girl's eyes grew very large and round and her dark face took on an expression of great seriousness. "Oh yes, missy, I shure will."

That day everything held a special poignancy for Lorabeth, knowing it would be the last in the home that had sheltered her.

It was easy enough to plead a headache as an excuse to retire early. As she went up the steps to her bedroom, she paused in the curve of the landing and looked back toward the parlor, where she could see Betsy chatting with Aunt Laura as she bent over her embroidery frame. There was a cheerful fire crackling in the fireplace, sending out a mellow glow on the polished furniture, and touching the brass candlesticks, the bronze and gold flowers in the blue pottery bowl.

A lump rose in Lorabeth's throat and she closed her eyes for a moment to memorize the scene. *When I am very old*, she thought, *with only my memories to comfort me, this picture will come to me.* It would be a precious reminder of a time she had first known the meaning of home.

Chapter 15

The next morning, Lorabeth eased her way down the back stairs of the slumbering Barnwell household. She was almost overcome by her feeling of sorrow. Valiantly she blinked back her tears and went out through the kitchen door Odelia had left unlocked, hurrying through the garden to the road.

A thin veil of frost covered the ground, and

drifts of fallen leaves cluttered the path she took toward the Duke of Gloucester Street and the Raleigh Tavern, where she would catch the stage to Yorktown.

She felt a certain eerie similarity in this, not unlike the morning she had crept away from Briarwood School to board the ocean vessel for Virginia. She tried to check the feeling of desolation and loneliness that threatened to engulf her. The feeling of not belonging anywhere washed over her.

As the stagecoach rumbled through the sleeping Williamsburg streets heading out of town, Lorabeth leaned her aching head against the window, bidding a silent farewell to the pretty little town that had opened its heart to her. Her eyes blurred with tears as the coach jostled over the rutted country roads, passing pastures, stone walls, and white farm houses set against dark, green pines. Virginia! How beautiful it was, she thought, remembering how this same wild beauty had frightened her a little when she first came. Would she ever see it again?

Lorabeth sighed deeply, settling into the corner of the coach, drawing her woolen cape closely about her. She was experiencing the depths of loneliness, almost as painful as when her father had died. But what she now felt was different. Never had she felt a loneliness of spirit so overwhelming nor so deep.

She burrowed her hands into her velvet muff, unconsciously touching the small leather pouch inside to reassure herself. It contained all the money she had in the world—money, that in all honesty, she could not call her own, unless the recipient of a gift was the rightful owner. But what if that gift implied a promise? Ah, but at this point, she could not afford to split hairs.

To some, she knew, a betrothal ring was the outward symbol of the sacred vows of marriage, although not yet consummated. All Lorabeth could hope was that kind, compassionate Blakely would understand when he read her letter of explanation.

Somewhere she had heard the saying, "Desperate times require desperate measures." Surely her position was desperate. And even if Blakely were brokenhearted for a time, he would certainly come to agree that what she had done was for the best.

It had all gone so much more easily than Lorabeth could have imagined. In a few hours Odelia would deliver her letters—the first, to Betsy; then, the one to Blakely, in which she had enclosed the redeemable ticket for the ring.

Lorabeth's cheeks burned, remembering the humiliating experience of pawning her engagement ring. She had tried to maintain a dignified hauteur as the hump-shouldered little man with the twisted smile held his jeweler's glass up and examined her beautiful ring for an interminable length of time.

He had fastened a curiously, malicious gaze upon Lorabeth and, with a deprecating cackle, asked, "And why would such a pretty young lady wish to part with this lovely ring? Obviously it is a token of some sentiment."

Lorabeth had drawn herself up haughtily and stared back at him so steadily that he was forced to look away and mumble a sum he was willing to pay.

"But, surely the ring is worth twice that!" she had exclaimed indignantly. Inwardly she was trembling and uncertain, but she was convinced this seedy character was offering her much less than its true value. She made a motion as if to take the ring back and leave, when he reluctantly named a price somewhat higher. The amount was still less than Lorabeth knew it must be worth, but his offer would cover her expenses until she was aboard ship, passage paid, and with a little to tide her over once she was back in England. So in the end she accepted it.

Recalling the scene, Lorabeth shuddered, feeling again the shame she felt at trading such a tender expression of devotion of bright hope and affection for mere cash.

Lorabeth steeled herself to weakening remorse, regrets. It was fatal to look back. Looking back could be her undoing. She repeated her Scripture verse to stiffen her resolve. What she was doing was the best and bravest thing—the best for *everyone*. For Blakely as well. He was too good and fine to have a wife who did not truly love him. She must believe she had taken the right course of action. If she began to question any part of her plan, she would falter.

When the stagecoach from Williamsburg finally rattled to a stop, its few passengers, cramped and cold from the long ride, got out and hurried up the steps of the Inn just on the outskirts of Yorktown. Inside, a fire blazed on the wide hearth in the front room. The men went straight to the public room to warm themselves with a tankard of hot rum, while Lorabeth remained in front of the fire, holding out her numbed hands to its comforting warmth.

She looked around, trying not to reveal the anxiety she was experiencing. Eyeing her curiously was a stout, motherly looking woman in a ruffled cap, homespun dress, and apron.

Lorabeth knew it was not often, nor customary, for a lady to travel unaccompanied by either a gentleman or a maid. She must speak to her at once, Lorabeth decided, before she became suspicious. Gathering all the poise at her command, she approached the woman who was standing behind the high desk in the partition between the front and public room.

"Good morning, madam. I should like to have

a room for perhaps a day and a night, while I arrange passage on the next ship setting sail for England." Lorabeth lowered her voice significantly so as not to be overheard by curious ears, and told the woman in a confidential manner, "I am recently bereaved of family and seek only privacy and solitude while I await word of the ship's departure date. I will take my meals in my room, if that could be arranged."

A look of sympathy immediately crossed the woman's kindly florid face as she listened to the words of this pale and lovely young lady. For a moment Lorabeth, reading her sympathetic expression, felt a stab of guilt. However, in a way it *was* true. She *had* lost her family just as surely as in any sudden tragedy that might befall a person.

Lorabeth lifted three large silver coins from her purse, and was holding them in her palm as she spoke. The sound of silver clinking together brought an instant response from the innkeeper's wife.

"Of course, m'lady," she replied, bobbing a little curtsy. "We have three nice rooms in the front upstairs for special guests. As it happens, one is just turned out and ready. Come along. I'll show you." She took a ring of keys from her pocket and came out from around her slanted wood desk. "Have you any luggage, m'lady?"

"Only one small box—if you would be kind enough to have the coachman bring it in."

As she followed the woman up the narrow stairway to the second floor, Lorabeth breathed a prayer of gratitude for the ease of her venture thus far. The woman opened the door into a room, then stepped back for Lorabeth to precede her.

The room was clean and plain, with a wide pine poster bed, a little round table, two chairs, and a fireplace. There were two small windows set in dormers and the walls were of white plaster. Lorabeth stood in the middle, turning slowly around, as if inspecting it. In reality, she was mentally contrasting it with the pretty room at the Barnwells that had been hers, as well as the large, luxurious guest bedroom at Montclair. The thought of Montclair instantly brought the image of Cameron to her mind. What would he think or say when he learned she was gone?

"Will this do then, m'lady?" the woman asked, bringing Lorabeth slowly back from her painful memories.

It was impersonal, just a way-station after all, Lorabeth thought, and she nodded.

"It will do nicely, thank you. And how can I find a ship sailing within a day or two, and the name of the ship's master with whom to book passage?"

"My Tom will take care of it for you. I'll speak to him right away. And would you like tea brought up?"

"Yes, thank you, that would be lovely."

Suddenly Lorabeth felt exhausted, worn out from the last few days, the stress of the past few hours during her secret preparations and clandestine departure. Unwanted tears sprang into her eyes at the woman's kindness. She tried to turn away so as to avoid the sharp-eyed innkeeper's wife. But she was not quick enough.

The woman lingered, then said in a softer voice, "Would you be wantin' anything else then?"

"No, thank you. Just the tea," Lorabeth replied in a muffled voice.

"Right away, m'lady. Rest yourself now. I'll bring you word as soon as we can find out about your ship and passage." She went to the door then and with her hand on its latch, she spoke again in her rough country brogue. "My name is Sara Hutchins, m'lady. If there's anything at all I can do, you've only to ask." With that she was gone.

Lorabeth realized that somehow she had touched the motherly heart of the woman and in a way she was grateful. But she must be careful, she warned herself. It would not be wise to attract any undue attention to herself, even if it was compassionate.

All that long day, as Lorabeth waited for word of whether she could get passage on a ship leaving Yorktown soon, she was filled with an aching loneliness.

This loneliness was worse than any she had ever experienced. Often, when she had been away at Briarwood, she had known times of vague, empty longings—not exactly for her mother nor for the shabby little house they called home. Nor was it the same kind of pain she knew after her father died and she realized she would no longer be able to see or talk to him.

This was something deeper, stronger, more painful. This was an emotion Lorabeth knew would be with her for the rest of her life. It was the longing for something she would never possess— something she had only glimpsed and known for a moment of time—the fiery sweetness of a lover's embrace, the memory of a kiss that would burn her lips forever, the void in her heart that would never be filled. It was Cameron Montrose she was lonely for, whom she would go on missing and from whom she could never really run away.

Somehow the afternoon passed. It was a gray, overcast day with occasional flurries of drifting snow. Lorabeth had heard that Virginia winters were fairly short but severe. She also knew a moment of apprehension, recalling the seamen's talk on her first trip across the Atlantic last spring, that winter crossings were treacherous.

Desperately Lorabeth prayed that there would be no problem booking passage, that she could go quickly from this Inn, board the ship, and set sail. She wanted to be on her way before there was any chance of anyone tracing her here.

She had given Odelia strict orders to report that she had a sick headache and wished to remain undisturbed all day. But Lorabeth could not be sure that Aunt Laura, in her concern, might not tiptoe into the bedroom to check on her and find the bundled pillows under the coverlet. She had told Odelia not to deliver her letters until a full twenty-four hours had passed. She did not want to risk discovery of her absence until she had a day's head start. Her hope was that, upon reading her reasons for leaving in this manner, they would all understand and accept her decision and would not attempt to bring her back.

The day darkened rapidly, and a knock at her door toward early evening brought a rosy-cheeked serving maid with a tray of supper. Lorabeth ate hungrily of the vegetable stew with chunks of meat, thick slices of rough-textured bread, sweet butter, and a pot of tea. The meal did not compare with the delicacies of the Barnwells' table or the elaborate meals served at Montclair. But it was hearty and satisfying, and afterwards she undressed and climbed into the high bed.

Lorabeth did not go right to sleep in the strange surroundings, but lay wakefully wondering what was ahead of her. She could hear the noise, the laughter and voices floating up to her from the tap room of the tavern part of the Inn. Since this room was on the front of the house, there was a continuous sound of horses hooves outside as men came to spend the evening drinking and talking with neighbors—swapping news, gossip, and politics. In spite of the noise, Lorabeth gradually grew drowsy. Worn out by the travel, the waiting, and the stress of anxiety, she fell asleep.

Lorabeth awoke, shivering and cold. During the night the small fire had gone out and the quilt had slipped off the bed, and in the chill of the unheated room she shuddered. Reaching for her cloak, she drew it around her and huddled back under the quilt. The gray light of early morning sifted through the small windows, and Lorabeth was helpless to restrain the tears that slid down her cheeks. Somehow her situation had never seemed quite so bleak, her future quite so frightening or futile.

She dressed hurriedly, scolding herself for being weak, fighting the tears that came so easily. It was the waiting that was the hardest, she reminded herself firmly. Once you had made up your mind about something, it was best if you could go on and be done with it. Not that she could have arranged anything sooner.

Almost as if in answer to her impatient thoughts, there was a knock at the door. This time it was Mrs. Hutchins herself, bearing a tray of tea and cornbread and bringing good news.

"Tom sent a messenger into Yorktown early, m'lady, and we should have the answer back before evening. Last night he heard in the tavern that the *Mary Deane,* a British ship, was loading the last of its cargo yesterday and should be setting sail by tomorrow at the latest. The passenger list was not full, so he understood, and you should be in good luck, if it's in a hurry you are." She paused as if to give Lorabeth an opportunity to tell the rest of her sad story.

But Lorabeth, although she appreciated the woman's good-hearted sympathy, knew the less said, the less chance of revealing her true situation. She thanked Mrs. Hutchins for the information, and asked the good woman to let her know as soon as word came.

Now with the final arrangements set in motion Lorabeth was as restless as a caged wild thing. She moved uneasily around the room, stopping every so often to peer out one of the windows, as if by so doing she could hasten the message she was waiting to hear. Outside, a raw wind was blowing, whipping the bare tree branches. The few people she saw down below were holding on to their tricornes, wrapping their cloaks about them as they strained against the strength of the wind.

She had seen a Virginia spring in all its shimmering beauty; summer, with its lush fullness, its warm dusky evenings; and the glory of its brilliant fall. But she had never known a Virginia winter, she thought, and now would never know one. By tomorrow she would be on board ship, moving out of the harbor. When winter came, she would be on the high seas.

Late in the afternoon it began to rain. The endless day was spent in alternating desperate prayer and the reading of spirit-soothing Psalms. Even then, Lorabeth found herself pacing the length of the small room, unconsciously wringing her hands, her stomach knotted in anxiety.

At length she stretched out on the bed, allowing herself for the first time that day to imagine what was going on in the Barnwell household. By now they had discovered she was gone. She hoped poor Odelia was not being punished for her participation in the departure. She prayed they, Grandmother and Aunt Laura, would not think her an ungrateful wretch but understand that she had wanted to leave with as little distress to everyone as possible.

Her thoughts were jolted back to the present by a rap at the door. She bolted up as the round, rosy face of the little maid peered around the door's edge. "'Scuse me, m'lady, but Mistress says to tell you there's a gentleman to see you in the keepin' room and would you please come down."

The man from the ship's captain! Lorabeth hopped off the bed, smoothing her hair quickly, adjusting her bodice and skirt. Then she took her leather pouch of money, slipped it into her inner pocket, and hurried out the door.

Holding her wide skirts, she ran lightly down

the narrow stairway, wondering how much of her precious money would have to be paid out for the passage. The messenger and the innkeeper would also be expecting their share.

Downstairs in the front room, Mrs. Hutchins looked up from her tall desk where she was working on a ledger, and with the hand holding the quill, she pointed to a door at the far end of the room.

"He's waiting in there, m'lady."

"Thank you," Lorabeth said a little breathlessly and went forward to the closed door.

The room was in shadows. The autumn darkness had come early and the candles had not yet been lighted. Lorabeth saw the cloaked figure of a tall man, his back to the door. Standing in front of the fireplace, he blocked the fire's light.

She cleared her throat and began. "Sir, I understand you bring word of the availability of passage on the *Mary Deane* and I—"

But he neither answered nor did she ever finish her sentence.

The man turned around, and in a startled flash of recognition, Lorabeth gave a muted cry. Her head spun dizzily and her knees buckled, and she would have surely collapsed had she not been caught up in two strong arms and lifted into an ardent embrace.

"Oh, my darling," the beloved voice whispered against her cheek as his familiar lips kissed her temple.

"Cameron! Oh, Cam, how did you know? How did you find me?" Lorabeth found her voice at last and it was a moan of anguish, and joy.

He held her tighter still. She could feel his strength flowing into her as he drew her more closely to him.

"Did you really think I would let you go?"

Chapter 16

They kissed again with all the eager intensity that separation and reunion induced. They said all the little loving, inconsequential things reunited lovers say as they clung desperately to each other.

At last Cameron kissed away Lorabeth's tears.

She leaned against him weakly, murmuring, "Oh, Cam, now it will be all the harder to part!"

"You're wrong, Lorabeth," he said tenderly.

"We won't be parting. I'll never let you go—not now, not ever."

"But, Cam—how can that be?"

"Listen, my darling. I'll tell you how it's going to be."

Lorabeth listened, wide-eyed, as Cameron told her how Blakely had ridden out to Montclair as soon as he had received her letter breaking their engagement and enclosing the pawn ticket. Then, as kindly as he could, Cameron confessed his own love for Lorabeth, and his certainty that she loved him in return. He then told his friend that he intended to go after Lorabeth and somehow to work out their problems so that they could marry.

"Blakely Ashford is a real man and a gentleman as well," Cameron told Lorabeth with genuine admiration. "I only hope I would have taken such a blow in the same honorable way had I been in his boots." Cameron shook his head. "If I've learned anything from all this, it's how to pray! I had to be brought to my knees, I suppose, to the point of accepting that I was going to lose you—if *that* was God's will for our lives. If your marrying Blakely *was* the right thing. I learned it wasn't right to 'bargain' with God nor to make your own personal happiness override honor. Thank God, I did not succumb to the temptation simply to kidnap you and impose my own desire above everything else."

Cameron stopped and smiled wryly. "I learned the hard way God's ways are not our ways, but that He 'works in mysterious ways' to bring about His purposes. Well, to go on with my story, I rode into Williamsburg and found the Barnwell household in a fine state of upheaval at their discovery of your disappearance.

"Furthermore, additional information concerning you has come to light, and we have Aunt Laura to thank for it." Cameron spoke in a decidedly firm tone of voice.

"What no one seemed to comprehend at first after receiving Aunt Winnie's letter was that if you are *not* Aunt B.'s *real* granddaughter, and no real kin to the Barnwells, then *we*—you and I—are *not* cousins!"

At this point Cameron leaned forward and kissed the lips Lorabeth had parted in astonishment, as she realized that neither had *she* fully comprehended that aspect of the shocking news of her parentage. Speechless, she listened as Cameron continued.

"Besides that bit of *very important* information, there is more. It seems, dear Lorabeth, that we are not even remotely related, as it turns out. My family has always accepted that my grandmother, Noramary Marsh's mother, was a *half*-sister to William Barnwell, Winnie and Aunt Laura's father. Well, the truth of the matter is they were *step*-brother and sister. William's father married a young widow with a daughter who was Noramary's mother. So there are actually no blood ties at all!" He finished with an air of triumph as though he were personally responsible for this amazing turn of events. "So, after all this, my darling, since there are no so-called 'impediments,' we can be married with the blessings of family and in the church as soon as the banns are announced."

Lorabeth simply stared at Cameron. She could find no words to express what she was feeling.

Cameron, clasping both her small hands in his, threw back his head and laughed uproariously.

"You don't have to say anything. Just kiss me again."

Lorabeth happily obliged.

After a bit she opened her eyes slowly and in their depths lurked a mischievous twinkle as she said lightly, "So, then, 'all's well that ends well,' is it?"

Cameron pretended to frown, then said ponderously, "Ah, 'so wise, so young, they say—'"

Lorabeth interrupted. "*Richard III*, Act 3."

Cameron struck his forehead in mock despair. "This woman I love is as bright as she is beautiful."

Lorabeth looked askance. "I don't know that one."

"I just made it up," Cameron grinned.

"It sounds as if it might be from *The Taming of the Shrew*, Lorabeth said thoughtfully.

"Then 'Kiss me, Kate'!" Cameron ordered.

This time Lorabeth offered no resistance. As Cameron's soft, firm mouth found hers again, she relinquished herself to the wild, sweet, soaring sensation. She had never imagined life could hold such bliss.

a month later

Aunt Laura adjusted the fragile lace veil over Lorabeth's shining hair, tucking pearl-headed pins into her piled up curls to hold it in place. Then she stepped back to survey her handiwork.

"You are simply lovely," she sighed to Lorabeth's reflection in the mirror.

Lorabeth, her dark eyes sparkling with excitement, smiled happily and, glancing over her shoulder, said, "Thank you, Aunt Laura. My hands are shaking so, I could never have managed it myself."

"Stand up, Lorabeth, so we can see if your dress hangs properly," Aunt Laura directed, trying to regard the slim young bride critically while all the time seeing her through a misty haze of tears. Although they were happy tears, still she did not want to spoil this day for Lorabeth with any display of foolish emotion. It was not always that such a love story ended this happily, she thought, remembering her own lost love.

Lorabeth stood, whirled around twice, her wide hoops lifting prettily. Her gown was made of creamy velvet, its deep, square-cut neckline edged with lace. Tiny bows of satin extended the length of the fitted bodice to the point where the velvet skirt draped back to show an underskirt of embroidered damask. Her feet were shod in pointed white satin slippers with roses fashioned of silk on the toes.

From downstairs they could hear the sound of the quartet of musicians tuning their instruments, and outside, the wheels of carriages on the crushed-shell drive as the guests of both the Montrose and Barnwell families arrived for Lorabeth's wedding to the oldest son and heir of Montclair.

"It's almost time," Aunt Laura said in a hushed voice.

"My bouquet?" asked Lorabeth, her heart

beginning a staccato beat. She had never dreamed the day would come when she would become a bride at Montclair.

"It's a very special one with special meaning. I arranged it myself," Aunt Laura told her. "Of course, I had the run of Noramary's greenhouse." She rustled to the other side of the room where she busied herself for a minute or so, then returned to hand Lorabeth a froth of starched lace with knotted satin streamers. Nestled within was a bunch of fragrant white lilies-of-the-valley, a single perfect white rose in its center.

"The lilies mean 'the return of happiness,' the rose 'single-hearted devotion,'" she said, smiling.

For a moment Lorabeth's eyes misted. Indeed, her happiness had returned, a hundred-fold. The impossible had happened, the dream she had hardly dared to dream had come true.

Escorted by her aunt, Lorabeth went out to the upper hall, stood at the balcony encircling the downstairs entrance hall, and at the top of the stairs she paused and looked down.

At the foot stood Cameron, handsome in a saffron velvet coat, buff-colored breeches, ruffled lace jabot, and satin waistcoat, his rich, brown hair smoothed back from his brow, his face turned toward her.

As Lorabeth started down, her bridegroom looked up. All devotion, all promise, all love shone in his eager eyes. Everything she had ever hoped for in life was about to become a reality.

The music played softly in the background as, step by measured step, Lorabeth Whitaker approached him. Three steps from the bottom, he went up to meet her, holding out his hand. She put her small one in his, and the look that passed between them confirmed all the vows they were about to make.

Family Tree

In Scotland

Brothers GAVIN and ROWAN MONTROSE, descendants of the chieftan of the Clan Graham, came to Virginia to build on an original King's Grant of two thousand acres along the James River. They began to clear, plant, and build upon it.

In 1722, GAVIN's son, KENNETH MONTROSE, brought his bride, CLAIR FRASER, from Scotland, and they settled in Williamsburg while their plantation house—"Montclair"—was being planned and built. They had three children: sons KENNETH and DUNCAN, and daughter JANET.

In England

THE BARNWELL FAMILY
GEORGE BARNWELL first married WINIFRED AINSELY, and they had two sons: GEORGE and WILLIAM. BARNWELL later married a widow, ALICE CARY, who had a daughter, ELEANORA.

ELEANORA married NORBERT MARSH (widower with son, SIMON), and they had a daughter, NORAMARY.

In Virginia

Since the oldest son inherits, GEORGE BARNWELL'S younger son, WILLIAM, came to Virginia, settled in Williamsburg, and started a shipping and importing business.

WILLIAM married ELIZABETH DEAN, and they had four daughters: WINNIE, LAURA, KATE, and SALLY. WILLIAM and ELIZABETH adopted NORAMARY when she was sent to Virginia at twelve years of age.

KENNETH MONTROSE married CLAIR FRASER. They have three children: KENNETH, JANET, and DUNCAN.

DUNCAN married NORAMARY MARSH, and they had three children: CAMERON, ROWAN, and ALAN.

Jane Peart, award-winning novelist and short story writer, grew up in North Carolina and was educated in New England. Although she now lives in northern California, her heart has remained in her native South—its people, its history, and its traditions. With more than twenty novels and two hundred and fifity short stories to her credit, Jane likes to emphasize in her writing the timeless and recurring themes of family, traditional values, and a sense of place.

Ten years in the writing, the Brides of Montclair series is a historical, family saga of enduring beauty. In each new book, another generation comes into its own at the beautiful Montclair estate near Williamsburg, Virginia. These compelling, dramatic stories reaffirm the importance of committed love, loyalty, courage, strength of character, and abiding faith in times of triumph and tragedy, sorrow and joy.

THE SAGA CONTINUES!

Be sure to read all of the "Brides of Montclair" books, available from your local bookstore:

Valiant Bride

To prevent social embarrassment after their daughter's elopement, a wealthy Virginia couple forces their ward, Noramary Marsh, to marry Duncan Montrose. Already in love with another, Noramary anguishes over submitting to an arranged marriage.

Ransomed Bride

After fleeing an arranged marriage in England, Lorabeth Whitaker met Cameron Montrose, a Virginia planter. His impending marriage to someone else is already taken for granted. A story of love, conscience, and conflict.

Fortune's Bride

The story of Avril Dumont, a wealthy young heiress and orphan, who gradually comes to terms with her lonely adolescence. Romance and heartbreak ensue from her seemingly unreturned but undiscourageable love for her widowed guardian, Graham Montrose.

Folly's Bride

Spoiled and willful Sara Leighton, born with high expectations, encounters personal conflicts with those closest to her. Set in the decades before the War Between the States, the story follows Sara as she comes under the influence of Clayborn Montrose, scion of the Montrose family and Master of Montclair.